Frozen Fire

Cadillac Press

Cadillac Press
185 Drummond St. Rd
Drummond, NB E3Y 1V9
Canada

Cover image by Angela Waters

2 4 6 8 10 9 7 5 3 1
FIRST EDITION THIS PUBLISHER

This book is dedicated to my Dad, who taught me to never give up.

Frozen Fire

Wendy L. Koenig

Chapter 1
Business As Usual

Torenz propped his feet on a tiny desk and leaned back in his chair, the springs in the old metal frame squawking in complaint. His fingers were laced behind his head and his eyes were closed. In his mind, he listened to the thoughts of a man thousands of miles away and nearly 1,940 years into the future.

"Twenty-seven equals D. L is...Y."

The man in the future, a telepath planted among the Allied coders of World War II, paused in his thoughts, so Torenz scribbled what he'd heard onto the yellowed notepad on his lap. The man began writing code again.

"Seven not procee—" The voice faded.

Torenz shoved his feet against the desk and rolled his chair across the dingy room, close to the giant violet wormhole that nearly covered one wall. The other telepath was weak, and the anomaly was damaged, getting worse every day. Proximity helped. As he closed on it, his skin tingles increased to the point they became painful. The smell of ozone stung his nose, making him want to sneeze.

The telepathic connection strengthened with the future again. *"—by alternate even number...A. The Nazis will never break that one on their own."*

Sneering, Torenz wrote the last bit of code in his notebook. The Allied commanders all foolishly believed that, somehow, the Nazis had managed to break every code they'd ever written.

It wasn't the Nazis.

It had always been him and his telepathic contacts stealing the code right out from under the Allied noses. He'd send it to his boss in the far future, who in turn would send it back through time to the Nazi war command.

He had other contacts in WWII too. Officials were still trying to figure out if John Cairncross was the fifth of the famous Cambridge Five spies. They couldn't make a solid connection between him and the Soviets. The truth—Cairncross was one of Torenz's.

No one believed in telepaths.

Even if they did, they'd never catch Torenz where he hid.

With a deep sigh at the idiocy of men, he cut the connection between himself and the coder and rolled back to his desk, lessening the effect the wormhole created on his skin.

He reached again into the future with his mind, but much further than World War II. It only took a split second to find the telepath in his employer's office and form the link between 1 AD and the end of the 21st Century.

Chapter 2
A Good Day Spoiled

In the 21st Century, jagged spears of indigo and violet snapped from the far end of the GlobeX lab where a massive wormhole dominated a brightly lit room—a giant silver whirlpool tipped on end. The closer Denefe came to the rift in time, the more the rift spiders—skin pricks from the collision of the Then and the Now—tingled under her skin. She felt as if she held the whole universe against her body.

The other GlobeX resident telepath, her boyfriend, Ardense, gave her a deep smile. His chocolate-colored hair was tousled and dark circles underscored his haggard brown eyes. It must have been a long twelve hours. Tall and lean, he winked from over the small knot of people changing shifts.

She hesitated and then returned his smile. Motioning toward the silver rift with its lightshow, she asked, "How long has it been throwing these sparks?"

"For a couple of hours now. It's been fun collecting reports. Staphershire hasn't checked in yet. I've been trying to reach him, but..." He shrugged. "It's been seven hours."

He unpinned the silver "On-duty Telepath" badge and then handed it to her.

Denefe shook her head. "I sure hope he hasn't done anything stupid. Again."

Reflections of the rift's sparks strobed across the silver of the badge in a purple and blue cloudburst. She traced her thumb over the three rippled circles etched below the word "Telepath." At seventeen, she was one of the leading telepaths with GlobeX. Yet, the emblem didn't soothe her anymore. They reminded her of how most people only saw her as a telepath. As if that was the core of her existence.

She jerked off her jacket and then tossed it onto an open desk. It was ridiculous to wear a uniform when there were no higher-ups present. Pinning the badge to her shirt, she jutted her chin toward the colorful offshoots from the wormhole. "They bring on any spikes?"

Though gravelly from exhaustion, Ardense's voice was tense when he answered, "A few small ones, but nothing dangerous this time."

Denefe pressed her lips thin. It was only a matter of time before another big one hit. Hopefully, it wouldn't be one of the sidewinders that snatched up people across the globe. "Okay then. Time for me to get to work. And time for you to sleep away the day."

His telepathic voice filled her mind. *"I'll be glad when they send someone for the third shift."* He gave her severe ponytail a tug, sending her long, white hair cascading around her face. As he exited the room, tucking her hair clip into his pocket, he turned back to her and grinned. *"See you in twelve hours."*

He rounded the corner and was gone.

Her team settled into their stations, and Denefe

12

faced them, opening her mind to read their non-telepathic thoughts. She sent to them, *"Sound check. How's everyone doing today?"*

They all answered at once.

"Fine."

"Good."

"Had better. My wife wants a divorce." Mik was her chief engineer. He mapped all the anomalies, as the scientific types liked to call the wormholes, and spikes that originated in that area. He was the oldest person on the station, nearing forty. Lately, Denefe had heard his deep, booming laugh coming from someone else's quarters late at night.

She scrutinized him. He didn't particularly look upset, but the laugh wrinkles around his eyes weren't as pronounced as usual. His light brown hair was combed a bit more neatly too. Not his usual devil-may-care style. *"I'm sorry, Mik. More time for your projects, though, right? You feel up to this? Ready to go?"*

In answer, he nodded with a determined smile.

She rubbed her hands together, and said aloud, "All right. What have we got?"

Charisse, her primary computer analyst engineer, or CAE, said, "Picked up a few spikes in the main channel last night. Nothing happened, though. Alerted the Primary Hub at 0247 hours, and the BaBy links—excuse me—the Brazil Base links at 0249 hours. No activity since."

Mik spoke up. "Current readouts?"

"All dead center to the fourteenth degree."

Denefe nodded. "Keep a sharp eye. Is there anything else?"

As one, her team shook their heads.

"No? All right, then. Let's find our missing boy."

Charisse entered the sequence to monitor the rift and opened a link to Staphershire's time, which she passed off to a secondary CAE. She looked up at Denefe and smiled. "Secondary now has monitoring of all perimeter airtime. Main unit locked onto link with Brazil Base Oh-four. Currently monitoring for spikes. You may proceed."

Denefe wandered down the stairs from the platform through the center of the room. As she came closer to the sparking rift, a telepathic vibration became audible to her, something akin to air blowing softly across the top of a bottle. Soft buzzes and pops came from the lightning-like spears of indigo and violet.

She walked past the rift to stare out the window at the canopy of her rainforest. The multiple shades of greens blended together below to give her the sense of a rolling sea. A low cloud shrouded the tips of the mountains in the distance, making them look like islands. Her body ached to go for a run today, and her mind craved the quiet it would afford her. Rainy season would be there soon. She should enjoy the outdoors as much as she could.

Behind her, Mik said, "Denefe, we're ready for you."

She faced the room, already focusing on Staphershire's personality, tracing what she knew of it all the way through the wormhole and back to the real person and into his mind. Not for the first time did she think it was like following a road through a tunnel. The way was a clear-cut path.

"Starry Boy, you there?"

Silence.

Chapter 3
Sidewinder

Denefe closed her eyes from the distractions in the room—sparks from the wormhole popping, feet shifting, fingers tapping on keys, even the breathing of her teammates. She strengthened her telepathic link to the past and called again, *"Staphershire, answer me."*

"Where has everyone been?"

He sounded too contrite, too…nice. That wasn't the Starry she knew. *"Why did you miss roll call?"*

"I didn't. I thought you did. Maybe the telepath wasn't strong enough."

"What were you doing?" Denefe opened her eyes and paced in front of the window. Outside, the rolling green ocean beckoned, speckled with violet and indigo reflections. She tightly pressed her lips together. Why was he stalling?

"Doing? Nothing."

Nothing? Not a chance. *"I repeat the question. What were you doing?"* Bright violet flashed against the window in response to a large mass of sparks behind her.

From across the platform, Charisse interrupted. "We've got a spike."

Denefe turned toward the room to watch her team. She wasn't worried, though. Her engineers would warn her if the spike caused any problems. It was the main reason they were there. They busied in the background, behind her telepathic conversation, diving into their individual tasks, keys tapping.

"Initial link to BaBy Oh-four solid," the secondary CAE added.

Staphershire said to Denefe, his "voice" sullen, *"You know where I am. The Roman invasion was the single most decadent era in our world's history."*

Denefe frowned. This whole tantrum of his was getting on her nerves. Like a parent of a misbehaving toddler, she forced an even calmness into her telepathic voice. If Starry had screwed up anything…

"We have the Temporal Accord for a reason. What were you doing? You start messing around and you'll screw up something in the timeline. Am I clear on this?" The mass of violet and blue spikes built into what looked like a huge thundercloud.

Mik punched up a grid on his keyboard. "Got the spike. It's a big one."

"I'll be good."

"You'd better be." She rubbed her temples. What was she going to put in her report? Experience had shown GlobeX that three strikes were too many excuses for some time researchers. After one mistake, like Starry's, the main office got trigger fingers. If he even looked at someone sideways, they'd pull him out of the program so fast he wouldn't know what time zone he landed in. *"I'll downplay this as much as possible, but it will have to be reported this time. You're a good man and right for the job. Just stay out of trouble."*

16

The rift spiders sharpened on her skin, and she snapped her head up to warn her crew even as she heard the secondary CAE say, "Showing a few transverse lines. We'll have to cut the link."

Denefe nodded. *"Starry, my friend, gonna shut down for a minute. Major spike coming. Clear the area, but don't go too far. I still need your report."* She cut the connection to him and nodded to Charisse. "Clear."

The woman tapped out commands on her keyboard and shifted the graph on her computer to include all mapped time.

"There she blows." Mik's voice underplayed a second hum that was now audible. The vibrations filled the room for a full five seconds. After they cut off, only the original telepathic rift spiders were left, biting Denefe's skin. The sparks were gone, leaving the wormhole as solid silver.

"Did we get it? The boys at Primary Hub would like a new spike to map." She walked to Mik's station.

He shook his head, pointing at the three-dimensional diagram on his computer. It showed the original rift in bright blue and the second wormhole in red, with one end clenched around the first like a snake. It stretched diagonally away, sketchy and wildly sporadic. "Sidewinder. It'll take me half a tic to figure out where it hit. You should be safe to go back in, though. If you make it short…" As his attention focused, his voice faded.

Denefe turned to Charisse and nodded.

Once the connection was re-established, Denefe said, *"Staphershire?"* Hearing no answer, she tried again. *"Starry, you there? Answer me."*

Mik's voice broke in, horror laced through it. "Our sidewinder hit BaBy Oh-four."

Denefe held Mik's gaze while she called Staphershire again. When she received no response, she shook her head. While Mik informed Port—the GlobeX authority on station—she kept trying to reach anyone at the BaBy Oh-four facility.

Within minutes, Ardense showed up at the door, rubbing his eyes and yawning. On his heels came Port, charging across the room like a bull released from a chute.

She put up her hand to halt him and shook her head. "No. Absolutely not. He just got off duty. He can't go. You'll have to go alone."

Port stabbed his finger at her. "*He's* not going. *You* are. He's covering your shift. If you don't like it, you can complain to the chiefs when we get back. Now, get in costume." He pivoted on his heel and marched out of the room.

"Oh, I intend to complain about a lot of things." She snatched up her jacket and left the room for her quarters. It was no secret she and Port didn't get along. Lately, he'd been baiting her at every turn. Really, how long were they expected to operate with only two telepaths? Out of all the people in the world, was it so hard to find someone telepathically strong enough to handle the station?

Denefe rushed to her quarters. Her complaint would have to be after her return from 116 AD. Checking the time, she found it would still be a few more hours before her twin, Kaleen, woke up where she was stationed. She really needed to blow off some steam, and her sister was usually more than happy to listen. Especially when it came to Port. She hated him as much as Denefe did. Actually, Kaleen hated everyone who represented GlobeX.

Denefe pulled on the traditional flowing white *stola* and then laced up her sandals. She coiled her hair on top of her head before she stood in front of a mirror to adjust a shawl-like *palla* to cover her white locks. No need to

18

give herself away. Her tanned skin and brown eyes would almost blend in with the local people. She went back to the control room to wait.

Ardense and Mik were studying the charts when she entered. Ardense looked up at her, pursed his lips, and nodded. She smiled at his approval, but the familiar unease filled her. It had started the moment he'd said he loved her and floated to the surface whenever he acted proprietary or came close to saying those words again. Did he love her, her abilities, or her looks? Would she always feel that way?

Port came up behind her, and she turned to see he'd chosen the typical middle-class toga. He said nothing, but jabbed his thumb toward the wormhole. Time to go.

Denefe followed him down the stairs and then stepped into the time rift. Just as she was snatched away, Ardense gave Denefe a nod. *"I'll listen for you. Good luck."*

Chapter 4
Starry Pursuit

Denefe had forgotten how much she hated time travel. It felt like being sucked into a giant vacuum cleaner. It twisted and pinched her body in ways and places that couldn't normally be reached. Her stomach pitched at the wild motion, and she struggled to hold onto her Eggs Benedict, regretting the vanity of her breakfast. Just as bile rushed to her mouth, burning her throat on its way, the rift spit them into Egypt, 116 AD of the Roman Empire.

They were in a wing, or *ala*, off the atrium of a house that GlobeX had authorized the first posted telepath to build. Sucking in deep, shaky drafts of air, she moved aside the ornate wall hanging that hid the wormhole.

The shallow pool called an *impuluvium*—if Denefe remembered the name correctly—directly in front of them had no central support columns to hold up the roof. That was unknown technology in that day and age. Across the water from where she and Port stood, sat a long, white reclining bed. It didn't look used, so she could only assume it was placed there for a symbolic meaning, as many things were in that era. Beside it sat a bust of Staphershire.

Being good. Indeed!

The back of the atrium opened into another open-roofed room. Curtains were drawn back on either side of the doorway. Seeing the lush garden inside, she decided that would be the *peristylium.*

She counted five adjoining rooms that appeared to be slave's quarters, and seven more that looked to be bedrooms with small personal servant antechambers attached. One room had thick, black smoke curling from out of the doorway. Reasoning it must be the kitchen, Denefe pointed at it, and said, "I'll check this end."

Port nodded and split to the other direction.

As she walked, she peered behind large potted plants and around corners into rooms. She saw nobody until she reached the kitchen. Flames leaped high out of a deep pot on a fire, scorching the ceiling. Dark, acrid smoke rolled the length of the room, disappearing out of the top of the doorframe and window. After lunging for a rag on a shelf at the side of the room, she wrapped it around her hands and grabbed the burning pot. Coughing and keeping her head back, she carried it to the window and threw it onto the ground outside.

Pivoting away, she came face-to-face with a charred lump that could only be a body.

Denefe's stomach clenched, bile again rising to her throat. The body—if that was what it could be called—had been roasted to a bright red, and all the skin had been stripped off. It was swollen and distorted somehow, as if the bones had been crushed. Lipless teeth grimaced at her beneath lidless eyes. The nose was a bulbous blister, centering the swollen face. Was this Staphershire? Or an unlucky slave cook? She'd never met Starry in person, but she thought he was smaller than the body in front of her.

GlobeX would send people to make a full investigation now that they had someone dead on the scene. Her job was finished as soon as she checked the rest of the house. She started to leave, but paused and turned back. He couldn't be alive still. Could he? After all that? She frowned, but couldn't make herself walk away. What if…? Creeping forward, inch-by-inch, she leaned toward the body. She didn't see him breathing. Was it even a him? She couldn't tell if the cook had been a male or female. Panic swarmed her. It became all important for her to know that detail. The person was dead, and she didn't know if it was a him or her. Biting her lip, she leaned down and reached for the cook's jugular. She wasn't going to relish placing her hands on the swollen, red throat.

"What are you doing?" Port's voice sent her pulse skyrocketing, and she shrieked, whirling to face him. She tripped on the body's ankle and fell in a sprawl on top of the cook. Shrieking again, she bounded up and away, against the wall, staring at the corpse. She almost expected it to get up and berate her clumsiness.

Port's laughter invaded the room from the doorway. She refused to look at him. Instead, she squatted beside the cook and placed her fingers on his…her…neck, checking the pulse. Nothing. She shifted her position, pushing against the red skin one more time. Still nothing. Disappointment at not knowing anything about the person flooded through her. Sighing, she stood and turned around. Only then did she look at Port.

He wiped his eyes on his sleeve, his face red, a teeth-baring grin on his face. She walked to him with a measured pace. Keeping her voice low, she said, "I'm glad I keep you amused."

His face became a stormy glare, even as he turned

away. She followed him out of the room, but turned in the opposite direction from him. There were still several doors around the *peristylium* to check.

"Denefe, you there?" Kaleen's telepathic voice sounded weak from that time distance.

"Good morning, sister mine! You're up early."

"Couldn't sleep. I'm headed out to the dig in a minute. You sound tense. Problems?"

Denefe moved around the edge of the *peristylium* to continue her search. *"Of course there're always problems with Port. We got hit by a sidewinder down here. It looks as if it took out everyone in BaBy Oh-four."*

"Everyone is gone?" Kaleen's words were thick with shock.

"We're checking now. It doesn't look promising."

"I didn't know anyone there."

Denefe sighed. *"I did. Anyway, I'm back in ancient Egypt, Roman Empire, investigating. So, sorry if I get quiet periodically."*

"I'm sorry about your friends. Does the company know yet?"

"I assume Port told Cardenza."

She could almost see Kaleen make a face. *"Ugh. Cardenza. What a pompous idiot. Just like the rest."*

"Yep." Denefe moved into the atrium, and walked into the first doorway next to the *ala* where the rift hid. Photographs adorned every inch of the walls. Photographs? How did Starry sneak a camera in there? Further, how did he develop them?

"Yet you still like working for them?"

"Liking GlobeX has nothing to do with it. Working for them is a means to an end. I have plans for my future." Denefe touched the image of a woman reclining on a bed by the pool in the *impuluvium*. The paper felt like the common parchment of the day. When she

removed her hand, ink smudged across the photo. *"Besides, I intend to resign if they don't get Port out of my hair and get a third telepath assigned to our station."*

Starry could have had the photos made at a local printer's, but it was technology the Romans shouldn't have had yet. She looked at the other photos. They were all of women, and all of them had been on that bed. Starry hadn't been behaving at all.

"No! Resign? You? I can't believe it! Not Miss Company herself."

"Shut up, already! Do I need to remind you that you technically still work for them too?" Denefe grinned. She turned around and around in the room. There wasn't much of a place to hide things. So where was the camera?

Laughter rippled from Kaleen's mind. *"Yeah, but I don't have to put up with any of them. They just sign my paycheck. Out here, I'm my own boss. You should come join me."*

"I will, if I they accept my resignation. At least for a little while." In a basket near the bed sat the triangular wooden telepath's metronome. It was fist-sized and GlobeX green with their symbol embossed in gold on the front. She had an identical one at home by her bed. Picking it up, she immediately felt the odd weight of it. Maybe that one wasn't standard issue, after all.

Chapter 5
Secrets

Denefe couldn't see anything abnormal about the metronome besides the weight, but Mik would probably find the difference. She'd lay odds it was the camera.

Kaleen's light laugh rippled through Denefe's mind again. Her twin said, *"You have to find the dig first."*

"Hah! The laugh's on you. I already know where it is." Denefe reached the door and crossed into the next room.

"What?" Kaleen got silent.

Now it was Denefe's turn to laugh. *"I know everything you do. Last week, you dug up the fossil of an ancient frog. How it got there, who knows. I even know how often you eat fried eggs. I have friends in high places."* The room was empty, so she moved to the second.

Kaleen's voice scoffed at her. *"Low places, you mean. You know, they won't accept your resignation."*

"Maybe, maybe not. Either way, I'm taking a vacation. Let's meet somewhere." That room was also

empty. Denefe stood still in the center, staring at the floor, concentrating on Starry's personality again. She still felt no essence of him. Not anywhere.

Kaleen's voice filled with excitement. *"All right. Gimme a few days to coordinate things here. You think of a place, and no sports centers, either! You know I can't do that stuff."*

Denefe laughed again. *"Would I do that to you?"*

"Yes, you would. You did it last time. I mean it. No sports centers."

"Okay, okay. Don't take too long arranging things there. GlobeX probably won't let me have much of a vacation."

"I knew it. You really don't intend to quit, do you?"

Hearing a noise, Denefe lifted her head. Port moved into the doorway. He didn't say anything, just stared angrily at her.

She glared back, saying in her mind to Kaleen, *"I'll quit in a heartbeat!"*

"We'll see."

"Gotta go. Gotta deal with Port." Aloud, she asked her station manager, "Do you have a problem?"

"Ah, joy. Later!"

His voice ground out harshly. "Yes, I have a problem. I told you I would check these rooms. You're wasting time."

"Is thorough a waste of time?" She smiled sweetly and walked to the door.

He clenched and unclenched his jaw, the muscle bunching tightly. "It is when done under suspicious motives." Pivoting, he marched back to the atrium where he sat on the bed by the pool, waiting.

What a day! She was exhausted. Her quick search of the rest of the rooms revealed nothing. The burned body in the kitchen was the only one.

She went back to the atrium, and Port turned his

head away with a scowl. She said, "I didn't find anything. Assuming you didn't either, I think we can go."

He jumped up and strode quickly to their originating *ala*. She fought hard against the temptation to slow down just to spite him.

The trip back through the rift wasn't as hard on her as the first one. Though she did reaffirm her vow to never again have eggs before she time-jumped. When they arrived at the base, Mik met them, frowning with uncertainty. "Cardenza's been trying to reach you, Port. He sounds angry."

Port glared at Denefe. She shook her head. "It wasn't me. I couldn't have. I was with you. Looks like it's just your lucky day."

He frowned and picked up a quick pace to his quarters.

Mik turned to Denefe. "How'd it go?"

She shrugged. "Port was his usual charming self. What can I say? Any contact with Staphershire?"

"None. Cardenza asked if you'd gone on the investigation with Port. The boss didn't seem to like the answer."

Ardense joined them on the platform. "That's because I contacted him about the situation. This was way out of line. Port should have gone alone." He asked quietly, "How was it?"

"We only found one body. I don't think it was Starry, though."

Mik closed his eyes and swore. No one else in the room said anything. Denefe smelled something like barbeque cooking for the noon meal. Her stomach lurched, and the image of that burned corpse popped back into her mind. Maybe she'd go on a diet.

Mik klunked down the stairs to his station, frowning, and Denefe turned to her primary, Charisse.

"Any new spikes?"

She yawned and shook her head. Long strands of honey-colored hair fell into her eyes and she pushed them aside. "No, it's been quiet."

"No messages? No tasks? Nothing?" Her voice sounded dull, even to her. Starry was gone. Missing. Probably dead. That was what the sidewinders did. They killed people in the most painful ways possible—by tearing them apart. She'd never been close to death before. Except for her parents, of course. She'd been too young to understand it at the time.

"Nothing at all. It's still too early for second roll call." Mik's voice was subdued.

It always was quiet right after something major. A small consolation to those left behind. Denefe slowly went down the stairs, and walked through the center of the room to the window. Ardense followed. He put his arm around her waist, and they stared out at endless green ocean of the forest. She looked up at him. Dark half-moons hung under his eyes and his cheeks were hollow from exhaustion.

She said, "Why don't you head back to bed?"

"You should get changed first, though." He cuffed his hand around the back of her neck, pulling her to him. He held her for a long time, not saying anything. She knew what his thoughts were—it could have been her who had gotten hit by the sidewinder. He straightened and kissed her forehead. "Hurry back. I'm beat."

Chapter 6
Discovery

Kaleen tugged on heavy arctic boots over her triple layer of wool socks. She shrugged into her parka before she pulled her alpaca mittens over a pair of thermal gloves. After opening the tent flap, she stepped out into the day. The cold snapped at her and the sun's glare bounced off the layers of snow, blinding her momentarily. She fumbled in her pocket until she found her sunglasses.

After she slid those into place, she automatically put her hand up, snagging the guide rope, even though she could see clearly all the way to her destination. One could never tell when a squall would dust up enough snow so a person could get lost.

Within just a few crunchy steps, she reached the first junction in the rope that divided people toward their private tents. The second junction sent a person to either the latrine or the dining hall, depending on the direction turned.

Kaleen went straight through, past the third junction

29

that split off left and right branches that led to the main office or Bridger Law's lab, respectively.

Her straight-on trajectory took her to the field tent, where she spent nearly all her time.

She opened the tent flap, stepping into the warmth of the anteroom and the bubble of her coworkers in various stages of dress. Most, like her, were just arriving, but a few—having found their digs still not thawed sufficiently from the night's freeze—were leaving to wait over another cup of coffee.

Before laying her coat onto the pile on the overburdened table set aside for just that purpose, Kaleen grabbed her tools out of the big pocket she'd sewn inside the parka. As she reached for the secondary tent flap, allowing her access to the field, it whipped open, and she took a quick step backward, sucking in her breath in surprise.

Bridger, the dig manager, seemed just as shocked to see her. He blushed and stammered, "I was…uh…just coming to get you. Your site's thawed."

Overcome with shyness, she gave him a half-smile, then ducked her gaze to the ground. "I'd hoped so." Lately, she just couldn't seem to look him in the eyes without becoming all girly-crush. She was conscious of his continued attention as she entered the field and walked to her site.

Yesterday, she'd discovered a broken human skull. Today, she started with her brush, working the packed dirt away from the orbital socket. Her specimen lay on its side, twisted, with its face buried in the ground.

The work was tedious and back-breaking. The body had been in the ground for thousands of years. More than once over the next few hours, she had to stand and stretch her spine. Each time, she found Bridger's gaze on her. The second he realized she'd caught him staring, he turned away and she returned to her work, smiling.

At last, she had completely unearthed the orbital socket. Male, she judged. Round ridges, such as the European ancestors had. So, a stranger in Siberia. That explained why the skull was crushed. He'd probably stepped on someone's customs, being an outsider and not knowing better.

She sighed and shifted her brush to clean the edges of the gaping hole in the man's skull. The bristles caught and then flicked a small piece of something hard onto the frost-hardened ground.

Setting her brush down, Kaleen picked up the dislodged piece. It wasn't a rock, but what was it? She turned it over and over. Her eyes widened and her heart hammered as she recognized what she held. "Bridger!"

Chapter 7
Sudden Appearance

Eight hours after Starry went missing, Denefe stared at Bade Hallen's flickering image on her com. He was a short, balding man who carried himself as if he were a giant. He said, "Denefe, I understand, but I can't do anything about Port. I've told you this every time you've called. When his and Ardense's complaints came in, they landed in Maurice Cardenza's lap. He's the one handling it. As I said, talk to him."

"I'm talking to you. I don't want to talk to him. What do you mean you can't do anything? You're his boss. Tell him to get rid of Port."

"Den, it's his investigation. It's not that simple—"

She gritted her teeth. "Yes, it *is* that simple. I can't work with Port anymore. Either he goes, or I do."

Hallen clenched his jaw and stared at her. He nodded slowly, his gaze never leaving her. "I can speak to him again. That's it. I make no promises." The screen went black.

Denefe sat back in her chair. Cardenza. It seemed as if her world was full of idiots. She'd wait to talk to him until after Hallen had time to correct the situation.

She rubbed her eyes and then sighed. She'd searched for Starry ever since she'd come back, calling for him every fifteen to twenty minutes. Her hope was that he'd used the distraction of the sidewinder to take off and would show up again sooner or later. Now that her shift was over and Ardense was awake and on duty, he was searching also.

Back to her research. She punched in her security code and then pulled up Staphershire's bio. His grinning picture met her. Bright smile, brown hair, blue eyes. Nice-looking.

"Raph Jones Staphershire. Male. Twenty-three. Registered telepath with a decent score—173.6. Is he married? Yes... No. Divorced. No kids."

Kaleen's voice filled her mind, interrupting her. *"Denefe."*

"Just a minute." She put her finger on the screen to keep her place while she read. "Father, dec—"

"This is important." Kaleen's telepathic voice was filled with anxiety.

Denefe dropped her finger. *"What is it?"*

"We found a body in the dig."

"So? Isn't that what you do?"

"Yeah, but it's one of our telepaths. From the past."

Denefe frowned at the empty air in front of her. Did she hear right? *"What?"*

"We found a computer chip in his brain."

"A what?"

Kaleen spoke slower. *"A. Com-pu-ter. Chip. You know, one of those—"*

"I know what it is. Do you know who the telepath was?"

"I've had to be careful and sneak around doing this. So it took a while. His name is Raph Staphershire."

A physical jolt of adrenaline ran through Denefe.

She jerked her eyes up to the screen in front of her. Raph Jones Staphershire? With a computer chip? *"He was at BaBy Oh-four."*

"So I found out. That sidewinder must have slung him way into the past, here."

Denefe stood, no longer able to hold still. *"I'm coming there. I need to see this."*

"I'd hoped you would."

"I just need to get permission from Cardenza." She grimaced. It looked as if she'd be talking to him, after all.

Kaleen's wry laugh echoed in Denefe's mind. *"Yeah. Good luck with that!"*

"Don't you worry. I'll get it. Talk to you as soon as I get the details worked out." She looked over Starry's bio again. Nothing to comment on, really. Just a good old boy who decided to have fun. She sighed and flicked the screen to Cardenza's line.

When he didn't answer, the call forwarded to his secretary—a prune-faced woman who Denefe felt sure had never smiled a day in her life.

"Mr. Cardenza is in a meeting. I'll give him the message that you called."

Denefe thanked her before she turned off the screen. She itched to get moving, but she couldn't until she had permission. Still, she had to do something. Looking around the room, her gaze lit on her metronome. She'd given Starry's to Mik immediately upon her return, but he still hadn't gotten back to her about it. Maybe she'd just go see him. Eager to be engaged in any kind of action, she nearly ran out of the room.

Mik's quarters were just down the hall from hers. Before she knocked, she leaned her ear against the door. Not hearing any noise, Denefe continued to Charisse's quarters at the end of the hall. Even before she reached it, she heard Mik's bass voice echoing against the walls.

She rapped on the door. "Mik. It's Denefe."

The room got suddenly quiet and, after a second, the door opened to reveal Mik dressed in Charisse's silk robe. He had a sloppy grin on his face. It seemed all his unhappiness of his divorce announcement that morning had disappeared.

"Am I interrupting?" Actually, she didn't care if she was. This was business. Behind Mik, Charisse peered around the corner at them.

"C'mon in!"

She shook her head. "I'm just checking on what you found out with that metronome."

"Ah, right." He turned to Charisse. "Be back in a minute, love." He stepped into the hallway with Denefe, pulling the door shut behind him. He led her to his quarters and then reached under the far corner of the foot of his mattress. From there, he pulled out Starry's metronome. Turning to her, he said, "Port's been asking about this, but I figured I'd wait to see what you wanted done with it. Took me until just an hour ago to figure it out."

Mik held the metronome close to Denefe's face. "You were right about this being a camera. Pretty ingenious, actually."

She nodded and tried to take the item from him, but he refused to let go. What was he waiting for? She hedged. "I was thinking the same thing."

"There's another thing with this too. It's got a small recorder device in it, voice only. That's the part I didn't want Port to find out about." He let her take it and pointed to a tiny hole at the edge of the gold GlobeX emblem. "See, that's the microphone."

Denefe frowned. "What was recorded?"

"Well now," he began with a skittish look on his face. "It says a whole lot that I'm sure no one at GlobeX needs to hear, otherwise, why would it be hidden? I had to use a translator on it because it's in ancient Egyptian. I only got partway through it, but I heard a few things that don't make any sense. You'll probably want to listen to that in private. I can stall Port for a few more days yet."

She nodded as he opened the door to the hallway and then escorted her out. He said, "If you need anything else, let me know." He started back to Charisse's quarters.

Denefe went in the opposite direction, toward her own rooms, but pivoted back, calling to Mik. "How do I turn it on?"

He turned around, walking backward toward his destination. "Push a needle or something small into the other hole on the bottom." He spun back before he disappeared around the corner.

She continued down the hallway, turning the metronome over and over. A recorder. What had Starry been doing?

Chapter 8
Bluff Called

When she reached her quarters, the live-call-waiting light flashed on her screen. The originating identity read, *Maurice Cardenza.* Lovely. She wasn't quite ready to speak to him. He could just wait a minute while she went to empty her bladder.

Returning, there was the flash of a second message waiting. She decided to read it first. It was from Mik, and not live. Unlike Cardenza's. She grimaced and read Mik's. *Forgot to tell you, only press the pin in the hole one time or you might erase some of it. Found that out by error. Sorry.* There was a smiley face, drawn by Charisse, no doubt.

Denefe carefully moved the metronome out of the viewpoint of her monitor and then opened the channel to Cardenza. Immediately, he lifted his head from his paperwork. Dark circles underscored his bright blue eyes and his lean face looked even more drawn and ragged than usual. "You called me?"

Everything she'd planned to say flew out of her mind. It always seemed to happen when she spoke to him. She didn't find the man attractive, nor was she in awe of him. If she was honest with herself, it was probably because he intimidated her.

He frowned at her silence and then said, "Denefe, if this is about Port, I still haven't decided what to do yet. I'll let you know as soon as I do."

There, that was it. "He's overstepping his boundaries—"

"He says you're overstepping yours." He raised his eyebrows.

Denefe dropped her jaw, feeling the heat of her anger flood into her face. "I'm telling you, he's behaving inappropriately."

"Well, that may be, but the fact remains that you have also. He says you're pushing him as much as you can, and that you're inciting the others to mutiny against him. Is that true?"

"What? You got the report from Ardense—"

"Yes, I got the report, but it means nothing. He's your boyfriend. Of course he'll side with you."

She couldn't believe what she'd heard. Could he really believe Port? "The others here will collaborate what I've said."

He nodded and drank from his coffee cup, a deep purple one that said, *Daddy.* He continued. "Which only goes to prove that you're inciting them. Denefe, I'm trying to keep an open mind. I'm trying to help you. Let it die down a few months, then I'll dig into it more."

"*A few months*? I don't believe this. I can't work with him for a few more months. Either you take him out now, or I'm quitting." She jutted out her jaw.

His face took on a dark scowl. "If that's the way you want it, I'll expect your resignation on my desk within the hour." The screen went black.

Denefe rocked back in her chair, shocked, numbly tumbling over the conversation again. That wasn't the way it was supposed to go. She sniffed and stood. At least she wouldn't have to worry about getting permission to go see Kaleen. Then again, once Hallen found out about her quitting, he would fix it so she could stay. It would be better for her future plans of her own telepathic relay company. She still needed more cash, but she wouldn't go back until Port was gone and a third telepath was posted.

She sat back down and punched in the link to Hallen's channel. Perhaps she could use this to her advantage. Hallen didn't answer right away, and adrenaline from her argument with Cardenza itched under her skin. She stood again and pulled out a travel bag. There wouldn't be much to pack. She'd given Kaleen all her winter clothes.

Denefe let the link to Hallen ring through, and by the time she had most of her underclothes packed, she was sick of waiting. She reached over to flick off the link, but his face showed just then, hand already raised to ward her off any arguments. "I know, I know. I've just been discussing the situation with Cardenza. Don't quit. Give us time to figure out what's happening."

She sat and ignored Hallen's placating gesture. "Cardenza has no idea what's going on here. I want someone else to head the investigation. I know those reports may look bad, but I'm telling you, Port's way in the wrong here."

"I can't pull him off the project, but I'll oversee everything he does. I promise we'll check into it. Give us time, okay?" He nodded, as if she'd forget herself and start nodding with him in agreement, his bald dome reflecting the room's lights as he moved. He'd spent too much time dealing with the government, she decided. His political techniques wouldn't work with her, not if he didn't get things fixed.

She set her jaw, and said, "We need that third

telepath. It's too much for only two. We need time off. I'd like to go see my sister."

"Certainly. I think that may be a good idea. Take a couple of weeks now. I'll have a telepath there within an hour. Tell you what, I'll even authorize you to take first class on one of the company shuttles. Okay?"

Denefe nodded. "Thank you." She sniffed. Funny how they were able to get another telepath so quickly now that she threatened to leave.

"Anything you need. Just don't quit on me."

"I'll wait to see how the investigation turns out, but I can't work with Port for months before you even begin."

"Fair enough. I'll see what I can do." He shut the connection.

Denefe stood and began packing again. *"Kaleen, you there?"*

"Here."

Folding a red shirt, she said, *"I'm coming up on the next shuttle."*

A pregnant minute passed. Kaleen answered, *"I guess I didn't expect Cardenza to let you."*

"He didn't. Hallen did, as a concession to me not quitting."

"Oh, I see. So you threatened him."

"No, I told Cardenza that I quit. Hallen stepped in and convinced me to stay until they could investigate." Denefe closed the compartment in her bag and then opened the next one. After walking to her closet, she pulled out two pairs of shoes and held them up. Which ones?

"Wow! You actually quit. I can't believe it."

"I told you." Shrugging, Denefe carried both pairs to her bag.

"Indeed. What good is a bluff if you're not willing to carry it through?"

40

"I'm not bluffing. They either get rid of him, or I'll make my resignation permanent." She jammed in the shoes, but the second one of the second pair just wasn't going to fit, no matter how she turned it. She jerked its mate out before she zipped the compartment shut.

"So Hallen approved the trip to get you to burn off some steam?"

"Yep." Denefe held up her heaviest T-shirt, unzipped the pocket with the shoes again, and stuffed it in. *"Gotta do some winter shopping before I get on the shuttle, though."*

"Yeah, you might get cold in just your uniform."

"Who says I'm wearing that?" She smiled, as if Kaleen could see her.

"You're taking a company shuttle. You're required to wear it."

"What are they going to do? Fire me?"

Kaleen chuckled. *"I see your point. I gotta run for now. See you soon."*

Denefe snatched up her jewelry and poured it into a side pocket. *"Absolutely. Wish me luck telling Ardense."* Suddenly apprehensive, she bit the inside of her lip.

"You haven't told him yet? Wow! I don't want to be in the same room when you do. Good luck."

"Yep. Talk to you later."

Denefe finished packing her last few shirts and then looked around the room. What else did she need to take? Her gaze lit on Starry's metronome. She had no time to listen to the recording now. Wouldn't it just make Port angry if she took that with her? She shoved it into her pack.

Chapter 9
Frozen Tundra

Within an hour, Denefe was on the rocket plane to the Siberian hub and Kaleen. She shifted in her seat, tugging on the cowl-neck of her brand new beige sweater. Bad idea to put on the winter clothes before she got to her destination. She thought she'd save time by dressing in the changing room at the station store. She tugged on the neckline once more and shook her head. Never again.

Ardense was sorry to see her leave for a few weeks, but he'd taken it well. It was her resignation that gave him plenty to say. They'd been in his quarters, and his voice had easily filled the tiny space and spilled over into the hallway for everyone to hear.

"I can't believe you did that! What were you thinking?" He'd stared at her with heavy, stormy eyes.

"I was thinking that I can't work with Port anymore." She'd shrugged and taken a step back, suddenly leery of the direction the conversation had been going. She'd made light of it, hoping he'd understand. "It's not that big of a deal. I'll find another job."

"As if Port's the only detail in your life right now?"

She hadn't said anything, though she'd been pretty sure it was required. The ever-present unease had grown within her.

"Denefe, if you resign, you have to leave, and you'll go alone. I can't leave here until my term is done."

"So?" She'd shrugged again.

"So, you're the only reason I'm here. I put in for this assignment to be with you."

"I don't understand why you're so upset. My resigning doesn't affect anything between us."

"Think. I still have three years on my contract with GlobeX. I *can't* just quit. When I'm done with this assignment, they'll probably ship me to Primary. You can't go there either. You can't go anywhere I'll be located. I might as well be a jumper, for as close as we'll be able to be to each other." He'd stood with his hands on his hips, his chest rising and falling in agitated breaths.

She'd stared into his eyes. That hadn't occurred to her. "I'm sorry. I…I didn't think about that."

"No, you didn't." His voice had been softer, and he'd reached for her hands. "I love you, Denefe, and I don't want us to be apart. We've planned our future together—our telepathic relay company, where to live, even a family."

She'd shaken her head, tears filling her eyes, the burr of disquiet small in her stomach again. "Hallen won't let me quit. He'll figure out something."

He'd pulled her into his arms and pressed her head to his shoulder with his hand. "I sure hope so." They'd stayed like that until it was time for her to go. She had almost said that she loved him. Almost. Instead, she'd gotten into the shuttle and ridden away.

Denefe sniffed and stared out the window at the clouds beneath the rocket plane, determined not to think about Ardense and his declarations of love. True, she'd been a little rash in her resignation, but it had made Hallen finally decide to pay attention. Perhaps he'd start treating her a little more seriously and get a third telepath for their station. Of course there was the remote possibility that the whole thing *could* go south, and she could end up looking for a new job. What would she do about Ardense then?

She rubbed her temples. It would be a few hours before they reached the Siberian Hub. She yawned. Maybe she'd take a nap.

She settled back in her seat and let her eyes close.

In her dreams, she faced a great swelling and swaying ocean. Lightning shot up through and from it, dancing into the heavens. A sudden strike wrapped around her neck, strangling her and pulling her down. Water closed over her, engulfing her. Deeper and deeper it pulled her while the multi-hued lightning continued. Every time it lit the tides near her, it tingled on her skin. She could no longer see the light above. Bubbles broke, burbling against her. They became voices babbling. The sound roused her out of the ocean, and out of her dream. She fluttered her eyes open.

The babbling brook had been people standing in the aisle near her seat. They all held traveling bags. She looked out the window. The rocket plane had landed already and had been towed into a parking hangar. On the ground, shadowed images scuttled around the ship, loading and unloading suitcases, guiding great fuel loading arms that swung from the ceiling. One wall of the building held a giant paned window with waiting people behind it. Even from that distance, Denefe could make out Kaleen's snow-white hair. She sent the message, *"I thought I'd have to take a transport."*

"Are you kidding? I hardly ever see you anymore. Do you think I'd let any second go by that we could be together?"

Denefe laughed as she stood with her bag and fell into the line of disembarking patrons. *"I'd hoped not."*

She stepped off the rocket plane and onto the flat, frozen concrete. The cold radiated through her tennis shoes as she walked to the reception area. *"Boots! I forgot to buy boots!"*

"No big deal! There are plenty at the camp. Even in our size!"

"Well, that's good. Which reminds me, can I borrow some of your clothes while I'm here? I only had enough time to buy a couple of sweaters and a pair of jeans."

"I brought a coat for you to wear too."

"You're a lifesaver!"

She entered the waiting area. Her duplicate, in a slighter build, stood at the front of the waiting crowd. She seemed oblivious to the men staring at her, their interest clear on their faces.

The moment Denefe pushed through the barrier, Kaleen flung her arms around her, smothering her. "Oh, it's good to see you!"

Denefe answered in her ear. "I know. How long has it been now?"

Kaleen pulled back and linked her arm through Denefe's, piloting her down the walkway, past the staring crowd. It wasn't every day that people saw a near-albino, especially one who was an attractive woman. To see two that were so alike as to be identical was downright jaw-dropping. "Since before you took the assignment at the training academy, that's for sure. What was that? Eighteen months before the BaBy hub?"

"Something like that, I think."

"So how did Ardense take your resignation?"

45

Denefe rolled her eyes. Now that she was away from him, her familiar unease about him returned. Did he really love her? "Don't ask."

After she finished telling how he'd reacted, Kaleen shook her finger, and said, "He's quite in love with you, you know. Don't you mess this up!"

Denefe tugged her own albino hair. "I don't know. Sometimes, I think he's in love with this. Or my abilities as a telepath."

"It's more than that. I know it is, and so do you. We'll talk more about that later." Kaleen hugged Denefe's arm. "How long are you here?"

"Two weeks, maybe more."

Kaleen let out a loud whoop, and the few people who weren't already staring turned to watch them. "Two whole weeks! It'll be just like old times, when we were both at Primary."

"Yeah, except it'll be cold."

"Oh, just outside the tents."

Denefe put on the coat and a pair of gloves. They went through the doors and into a semi-heated private skimmer dock.

Two rows in, Kaleen pointed to a brand new skimmer. Emblazoned on the side was a giant triple ring logo of GlobeX. "This is ours."

Denefe laughed as she got in. "This dig isn't a bit important to them, is it?"

"Well, it really is. Once they got past the initial 'No!' they began to see the potential of studying the impact our researchers had during their visits."

"Besides the new skimmer, you got all kinds of new equipment, I'll wager."

Kaleen nodded, piloting into the air. "You bet. I'm willing to bet they do the same thing with you." They moved out of the building and then flew in a northeasterly direction, the skimmer only a few feet above the frozen terrain.

"I hope so. It's a completely different scenario from yours."

"We'll see, but for the next two weeks, we won't think about it." Kaleen reached over and squeezed Denefe's hand.

Chapter 10
All In A Day's Work

At the appointed time, Torenz pressed the button on his remote and the wall in front of him dissipated. He crossed over and pressed the button again. The wall reformed. That little bit of magic never failed to make him smile.

He turned the corner into his office and then settled onto his desk chair, staring at the giant, violet anomaly, waiting with his legs stretched in front of him and crossed at the ankles.

Normally, the meeting started on time, like clockwork, but after twenty minutes, he decided his boss's telepath had to be in conversation with someone. Rather than interrupt—the telepath would contact him when ready—Torenz decided to pay a visit to Denefe.

He stretched his mind into the future along the well-worn path to her thoughts, but something was different this time. She wasn't where she was supposed to be. The way took a drastic right turn to another destination, one he knew well. She was visiting Kaleen!

A pleased smile stretched across his face. That could be fun, bouncing from one to the other, uncovering all their secrets as their conversations sparked their thoughts.

His boss's telepath intruded. *"Torenz, are you there?"*

"Of course."

"Sorry I'm late. I was called into a meeting with the powers-that-be."

Torenz had nothing to say to that. It wasn't as if he really cared, so he just waited, frowning.

The man in the future continued. *"We'd like you to follow the telepaths in the rescue attempt at Brazil Base Oh-four. They're en route now. Inform us immediately of everything they discover, no matter how trivial."*

"Is that all?"

"Look, don't downplay this. It's of the highest urgency."

Annoyed now, Torenz stood, glaring at the wormhole as if the other man could see him. *"I know my job. You don't have to worry."*

"Fine. Good luck." The telepath left.

Torenz rubbed his face, trying to rub the anger out of it. After everything he'd done for them, how could they think he wouldn't do his job? Those people really frustrated him. He dropped to the chair again, suddenly deflated, and reached for Denefe. Listening to her or Kaleen never failed to calm him.

Like a bolt out of the blue, he caught the tail end of a thought. *"Starry's body is here?"*

Immediately, he shifted his focus back to his boss's telepath, a man whose name he'd never bothered to learn. He barged right in, without introduction, not caring if the man was mid-conversation with someone in his own time. *"Staphershire's body is in the Siberian dig."*

How was that for not downplaying?

Chapter 11
Corpsicle

The terrain below faded from smooth, plowed tarmac to rough ridges of white and brown ice as they moved away from the Hub. The skimmer picked up a constant vibration. Kaleen glanced at Denefe with an apologetic smile. "You'd think with all the modifications and jumps in technology they'd figure out a way to make it so these things didn't do this."

Denefe laughed. "At BaBy, the canopy of the forest is so dense, we can pilot these above it. The trouble is when we hit a less dense part, we take a dip to the ground. We've wrecked a couple of skimmers that way. We're not allowed to do that anymore."

"No, I can imagine not. Look there." Her sister pointed at the range of mountains that jutted up sharply from the tundra floor. Long curls of snow blew off the top of the peaks, arching over the edge and down toward the ground. "In some places, that builds up a snow walkway from peak to peak."

"Amazing." Denefe looked at her sister. "You really

love it up here, don't you?"

"Yeah, I do."

"Not me. The tropics are more my taste." She looked back to the front, noting they were headed toward a dark speck in the white blanket of snow.

"Oh, *come* on! You live to travel. I can't imagine you ever settling down in one place for more than a few years at a time."

Denefe grinned. "It almost makes you feel sorry for Ardense, doesn't it?"

Ahead, the dark speck grew into a camp. Kaleen settled the skimmer down next to one of the tents. "These skimmers have been rigged with a special warming motor to keep the big block from freezing in these temperatures. Cool, huh?" She opened her door and climbed out.

Very cool, indeed. Denefe opened her door, and then immediately shut it again. In that brief split-second, the cold had snapped her breath away and shocked the skin across her face like a slap. She pulled the hood of her borrowed coat tight over her head, took a deep breath, rushed out of the skimmer, slammed the door, and ran to the black tent.

Kaleen was already busy inside, pulling off her parka. She laughed when she saw Denefe's face. "You look panic-stricken."

"I want to go home now. I've had enough of the cold." She followed her sister's example, pulling off her gloves and coat. They stood in a little anteroom between two sheets of heavy canvas lined with thick plastic. "This is where you live?"

Kaleen shook her head. "This is Bridger's lab. He just stuck his head in here and told me we're working on borrowed time with this body. I don't know how GlobeX found out. They don't want us messing with it. I just wanted you to see it before they got here to take it away." She gripped Denefe's arm and lowered her voice. "Something's going on here. Why else wouldn't they want us poking around?"

"I don't know." Denefe followed her twin inside the main part of the tent. She needed to tell her sister about Starry's metronome, but not there.

The interior of the tent was warmed by a large heater in the middle. Still, it wasn't warm to Denefe. Lights had been strung up in long strings along the ceiling. A medium-height, light-framed man with light brown hair stood hunched over a table.

"Bridger, I want you to meet my sister."

The man set down a piece of equipment and turned, pulling off his gloves. With a lopsided grin, he stretched forward his hand. "Hello, Kaleen's sister. Do you have a name, or should I just call you 'Sister Xia'? Mine's Bridger Law."

"I'm Denefe. Nice to meet you."

"Don't worry, you'll change your opinion once you get to know me."

She glanced at Kaleen, who smiled. She turned back to Bridger. "I somehow doubt that."

"Kaleen says you know this fellow."

"Yes, I do…did. We are…were…friends of a sort."

"There are some very interesting aspects to this." He studied her for a minute, then said, "It's different looking at the body of someone you know. If you don't have a strong stomach, you should go wait over there by the wall while I explain." He motioned to a chair on the far side of the heater.

Kaleen spoke up. "She can handle it."

Denefe nodded, though she wondered if she could.

He shrugged and turned back to his table. His voice was muffled when he spoke, and Denefe had to come around beside him to understand what he said. Starry lay gnarled in a semi-fetus position, one leg and the

53

opposite arm tucked. The other leg was bent back, and the near arm was flung outward as if trying to catch hold of something. The body, on the whole, resembled a freeze-dried mummy, but the facial features were unmistakably Starry's.

Bridger asked, "As I understand it, he got caught in a time flux of some kind, right?"

"That's right." She moved her gaze up to Starry's face. Like the cook, the lips were gone and his skin was red.

"Well, as soon as your sister found the microchip, I pulled our whole team together to dig him out of the ground as quickly as possible. Time is of the essence here." He took a deep sigh and then said, "You should know, the most singular thing about this, besides the microchip, is the damage to his face."

"What? The cook was damaged like this too."

"Like this?" He took hold of the out-flung arm and one knee and tipped Starry's body up on its back. There, the hidden side of the head looked as if it had been burned from the inside out. A gaping hole was where his ear had been.

She took an involuntary step backward, putting her hand to her mouth. "Starry."

Immediately, Kaleen put her arm around Denefe's waist. "I'm sorry. Sit down over here."

Denefe shook her head and swallowed. She moved back to the table again. "No. It's okay. I'm okay. Where's the microchip?"

Bridger glanced at Kaleen. "We, uh, took it out. I'll show it to you in a minute. It's my guess it was originally located right here. Then fell into the interior of the skull where your sister found it." He took his pen and pointed dead center into the missing part of the skull.

"So, you think it was the cause of Starry's dea…of

this damage? Can that be? I was talking to him when he disappeared."

He frowned and spoke slowly as if weighing his words. "According to my tests, he was still alive when he landed. He froze to death. I found ice crystals in his lungs, which means he was breathing at the time he came to Siberia."

Still alive? She didn't want to think about that. "Do you think the sidewinder caused the microchip to malfunction and do that?" She pointed to the missing face.

"No, I don't. You'll see why." He eased the body back down to lie flat, then led her to another table and lifted a small plastic box. Enclosed within was a piece of metal about the size of the end of his pen. "Do you see any damage to this?"

She removed the chip and inspected it closely. It looked perfectly fine to her. She shook her head.

"Exactly. I found nothing under the microscope either. This chip wasn't damaged. It seems it was functioning perfectly. Of course I won't be able to tell for sure until I can get it hooked up to the proper equipment."

No malfunctions. That meant the chip was supposed to do what it did. "So, Starry was snatched by the sidewinder and landed here. Either before he landed or after, half his face was blown off."

Chapter 12
Conspirators

Staphershire had died in agony, that much was clear to Denefe. She took a deep, shuddering breath. "So, you have the equipment to test that microchip?"

Bridger bobbed his head. "I do."

"All right. I vote we let the corporation have the body and let's not tell them about the microchip. I mean, it could have fallen out during the accident, right?"

He looked pleased. "I'm sure it must have." They turned and looked at Kaleen.

She held up her hands in denial, shaking her head. "Hey, you know me and GlobeX. As far as I'm concerned, that body is exactly as I found it, and no one has touched it."

"When are they scheduled to take it?" To her twin, Denefe thought, *"Kaleen, can we trust this Bridger fellow?"*

Bridger answered, "They should arrive any time."

At that same moment, Kaleen also answered, *"Absolutely! He's an old school chum."*

Denefe nodded. "We should probably leave. It'll look suspicious if we're here when they come. *I don't remember him.*"

"*He wasn't exactly part of the popular crowd.*"

"*Ah! Do I detect some sarcasm there?*"

Kaleen giggled. "*Just a bit.*"

"*When was the last time you had anything to do with him?*"

"*We've kept in touch over the years.*"

"*I just don't think that means we can trust him.*"

Kaleen gave a mental shrug. "*Too late now. Besides, there's no one else I'd rather have.*"

Denefe sighed. "*Okay, but let's be careful who we let know about this stuff. Reminds me, I have something to show you when we get back to your tent. Another piece of the puzzle.*" Bridger, can I help you pack up?"

He shook his head. "No, thanks. I have it all now. By the way, that's quite unnerving when you two just stand there, obviously talking to each other in your minds. You nod and have other mannerisms of a conversation, but there's no sound. It's just…odd to watch." He smiled an apology and ducked out of the tent flap into the anteroom.

Denefe grimaced. "*A bit outspoken, but he's a nice enough fellow.*"

"*Yes, he is. And trustworthy.*"

"*I hope so. He'll have to get used to us, though.*" Denefe held the tent flap open for Kaleen, and they joined Bridger. She sighed, remembering another tiny room. "This little chamber reminds me of an ancient Roman house. I had occasion to be in one recently."

Bridger straightened from putting his boots on and stared at her. "The *alae*. You were in one?"

She nodded. "That's where the accident happened. I had to go investigate."

He shook his head and picked up his things. "I

would have loved to have been there. You time jumpers amaze me. You see all these wonderful, historic things, and you just treat them as everyday, commonplace."

Kaleen spoke softly. "Not all of us, Bridger."

"No? That's a wonderful thing." He held her gaze a moment, then abruptly pulled his away.

Denefe looked from one to the other. Unless she missed her guess, there was more than just friendship sparking between them. She cleared her throat, and said. "As we get the jumps more and more mapped, we'll be able to send for historians and scientists to go places in the past and verify certain data. Carefully, of course."

"Of course." He turned to the tent flap that opened to the frozen outside, then turned back. "I'd like to volunteer to be one of the first to go to Pompeii."

"We'll absolutely put in a good word for you." Kaleen snagged her and Denefe's coats from their hooks.

"How soon will you have some results on that chip?" Denefe asked.

He shrugged. "As soon as I find some, I guess. It's not like a lab test that I know will only take seven hours to run." He left.

Not relishing going back out in the cold, Denefe turned to her twin. "How far is your tent from here?"

Kaleen pointed. "It's just across the clearing. Ready?"

"No, but let's go before I lose my nerve." Denefe picked up her bag, and they dodged out of the tent into the bitter cold outside. It slammed into her like a head-on collision, stealing her breath and making her eyes run. If it hadn't been for Kaleen's firm grip on her elbow, Denefe would have turned back to stay with Starry's body. Maybe even have spent her whole vacation in there.

Her twin kept one hand on a rope overhead and

propelled her forward. Twelve-foot-high drifts of snow mounded on either side of the path. Even with only one turn, it seemed like forever before they reached Kaleen's tent. Here, there was another anteroom, and Denefe stood inside by the doorway, rocking from foot to foot, her hands pulled up into her sleeves, bag at her feet.

Her sister was already pulling her coat and gloves off. She glanced at Denefe. "C'mon, goose! How are you going to get warm if you don't let in the heat?" She reached over and began to undo Denefe's coat.

"H...How d-d-do you do...th-this?" Denefe's mouth just didn't want to open.

Kaleen laughed. "I do it because it has to be done. It's spring, though, and it's warmer than it used to be."

"S-Spring? Hah!" Denefe put the tip of her glove into her mouth and pulled. Meanwhile, Kaleen tugged her coat free from her other arm. They switched, and Denefe bit the glove off her free hand while Kaleen undressed the free arm.

Denefe bent to remove her tennis shoes. It amazed her that Kaleen was the tough sister there and she was the frail one. Quite a reversal.

Kaleen nudged her. "Are you all right with those? Do you need help?"

"No, I'm okay." She jerked off her shoes and then stumbled to the heater. Her feet felt like icebergs. Standing on one foot, she lifted the other near the warmth. After a moment, she alternated. "I just don't know *how* you do this. I know I couldn't."

Kaleen shrugged and joined her at the heater. "I love the work. I'd rather do this than anything else."

"It's true. I haven't seen you happier. Of course," Denefe shrugged, "they say the insane are the happiest people."

Kaleen laughed again. "Well, that may be, but at least I don't work for GlobeX at the moment."

Denefe shook her finger at her twin. "Yes, you do. They're financing your dig. If they pull their money, you have to come back to work as a telepath. While you're here, you can pretend you don't work for them, but someday you have to return to reality."

"Wanna bet?" Kaleen's eyes sparkled, and she gave a sly smile.

Denefe gave a sudden gasp in understanding. "Bridger has made you an offer to join his team when this is done!"

"They called you the slow one. Look at you go."

"Well, I'm happy you're getting out. You were miserable."

"Thank you. I think I'll like working with Bridger. He's actually got quite an extensive and impressive team." She paused and then looked at Denefe. "Have you thought what you'll do if you end up looking for a new job?"

"Just apply to all the big corporations, I guess. My relay company still isn't funded enough to start." She laughed. "I'm not really trained for much else but what I'm already doing. I don't think it'll come to that, though."

"I don't either, but we'll see what we can figure out while you're here. You know, just in case. Anyway, tomorrow we can go look at the place where I found the body. Are you hungry? I have a few staples and a burner here, or we can go to the dining tent."

Denefe shook her head. "No food for me. I just want to stay here by the heater."

"I'll make you something, and you can eat it there." She brought over a chair and then rummaged through her shelves. Within minutes, she had two cups of instant soup heating on her burner.

While she was busy with that, Denefe called Ardense. *"Are you awake?"*

60

"I am now. What's up, Den?"

"Kaleen's making soup. I'm just warming up."

"Port's pretty pissed at you. I guess Cardenza or Hallen has berated him on his handling of the whole matter. He's been informed there will be a formal inquest."

"Cardenza told me they were going to wait."

"Apparently, Port said or did something that pushed it over the edge."

"Or I did when I threatened to quit," Denefe thought.

Chapter 13
Rift Spiders

Denefe spoke to Ardense at Brazil Base in her mind. She stared at the heating soup. *"So, Port's making your life miserable? I'm sorry."* She hadn't intended to make anything more difficult for Ardense and her friends.

"No, it's actually a good thing. He won't talk to anyone here. Mik swears you should have complained earlier. He also sent the message that he can't wait for much longer. Whatever that means."

She knew exactly what that meant. Mik was talking about Starry's metronome. Better to leave as many out of the loop as possible. It would be safer for everyone that way. She would show it to Kaleen tomorrow. Together they could puzzle out the messages. *"I have no clue."*

"Well, I'm just the messenger boy. How's your sister?"

"Just as dry as ever. Wonderful to see her, though."

"Good. Give her my love. I'm going back to sleep.

Love you."

"G'night." Once again, she felt herself holding back, uncertain. She loved him. That wasn't the problem. She'd rather be with him than anyone, and she wanted to spend the rest of her life with him. Was his love a true love?

She joined Kaleen, and for the rest of the evening, between cups of tea and soup, they chatted about old friends and old loves. At last, exhausted, they went to bed just before four in the morning.

By the time Denefe awoke later that same morning, Kaleen was gone. *"Where are you, sister mine?"*

"I'm in the dig. You should join me. It's where I found the body."

"Er, okay." Denefe looked doubtfully at the boots Kaleen had placed near the heater for her, not sure if she wanted to brave the cold so soon after waking. *"How about in a couple of hours?"*

"Others will be here by then. Now's the best time. We'll be able to talk."

"Well, there's nothing to be done but to join you." She pulled on her boots. *Are you going to come get me?"*

"Just follow the rope straight through the three junctions. No turning at all. You'll be fine."

"Be right there. Turn up the heater."

"Um, there's not a lot of heat in here, actually, but it is *warmer than outside."*

"How long are we going to be there?"

"As long as you need."

"Or as short?"

Kaleen laughed in her mind. *"Or as short."*

"All right. See you in a few. Straight through?"

"Yup."

After Denefe finished struggling into her coat and gloves, she took a deep breath. She stepped outside.

Immediately, the wind scooped between her hat and head, flipping her hood back onto her shoulders. She flailed around for a minute, but had no luck with grabbing it. Ducking back into the tent, she righted her coat, tying it tighter. She stepped back outside again.

Denefe looked up and grabbed hold of the rope, letting it run through her hand as she walked. It took her no time to get to the first junction. Just as she reached it, another big gust of wind sailed into her. It tugged on her newly-tied parka, and pulled it loose again. She let go of the rope and turned around to put her back to the assailing gust, holding her hood with both hands. The wind seemed to swirl around her, first coming at her from one direction and then another. She turned around and around with its changes, always trying to keep her back facing its force.

With one hand on her still-adorned hood, she reached for the rope above her. When her hand met only air, she looked up. Only swirling snowflakes greeted her. She looked back and forth, finally catching a glimpse of the rope and junction. Trudging to them, she found herself faced with another dilemma. Which way had she been coming? Which way had she been going? The wind whipped the snow around her, obscuring the tents, sifting flakes into her footprints, hiding them. There was no way for her to tell. *"Kaleen! Help me. I'm lost!"*

"Lost? How could you be lost? It's just a simple rope trick. Honestly, Denefe! What did you do?"

"I don't know, but I'm really cold. I'm here at one of the junctions, all turned around. The wind came and tried to take my hood, so I let go, and when I looked back, I couldn't tell where I am anymore."

"Fine. I'm coming."

"Thank you." Denefe felt miserable, and she let that creep into her voice. Maybe Kaleen would take pity on

her and not be upset. She kept her hand on the crossed ropes and turned around and around, trying to catch sight of her sister. She was edgy and anxious, as if she'd jumped right through her skin. Turning once more behind her, she saw Kaleen buttoning her parka as she approached.

The edginess Denefe felt exploded into rift spiders crawling inside her skin.

Something slammed into her from behind with the force of a speeding skimmer. It jerked her backward off her feet, snapping her head back and then forward, hammering her chin onto her breastbone.

"Denefe!" Kaleen's scream rocketed through Denefe's mind, and then everything was drowned out by the roar of a sidewinder.

A blast of fiery heat hit her, and she remembered Starry's burned red skin and his missing eyelids. Snatching the edges of her hood between her thumb and forefinger, she pulled it low to cover her ears and used the rest of her hands to cover her eyes, nose, and mouth. Her uncovered skin burned with intensity like none she'd ever known. She felt it must have been peeling right off her bones. She fought to bring her knees up against her chest. The force of the sidewinder pushed against her, as if intentionally trying to kill her. Little by little, she won her struggle. After what seemed like forever, she was curled up into a little ball with her head tucked against her knees to help shelter it.

She was in a vise-grip, being squeezed until her bones would surely become nothing but bloody pulp or jelly. Her intestines felt as if they would be pushed out like toothpaste. She thought her body was being turned inside out. The sidewinder jerked her in two different directions at once. If she hadn't been in a ball, she'd have been torn in half. As it was, twice it wrenched her knees away from her chest, partially uncurling her. Both times, she fought against the power of the sidewinder to curl again. The second time, she almost didn't succeed.

A third time, two opposing forces tugged on her, uncurling her all the way. That was it. Now she would be torn in half. The agony in her midsection was more than she could bear, and she opened her mouth to scream when suddenly it ended. The wrenching of her body, the engulfing fire, the deafening roar, the rift spiders, everything—all gone.

Chapter 14
Panic Drone

"Denefe!" Kaleen launched to where Denefe had stood just a moment before. Remnants of ozone from the sidewinder permeated the air, and the residual electrical charge raised the hair on her arms. Snow whipped around her on the wind, obscuring anything more than a dozen feet away. As for the rogue wormhole itself, there was nothing left. Nor was there any sign her twin sister had even been there.

"Denefe!"

She turned around and around, looking for any sign, any clue, that would tell her where the sidewinder had gone. If she had the equipment the big bases did, she might be able to track where her sister had been taken.

Bridger came up to her. "What's happened? I was coming out of the tent to stop you so we could speak when you ran away."

"Denefe! Where are you? Can you hear me?"

Kaleen crossed her arms and shivered from the fear that snaked throughout her, not feeling the cold. Not really seeing the man in front of her. All her attention was focused on one thing.

"Denefe! Answer me!"

"What's happened?" Bridger gripped her shoulders and gave her a small shake.

She croaked, "A sidewinder took Denefe." Her face twisted in grief. Try as she might, she couldn't hold back the sobs that suddenly lurched into her throat. Tears rolled down to her cheeks, turned icy, and froze.

He pulled her to him, wrapping his arms around her. "Hey. She might be all right. Your sister's smart. She saw what happened to that other telepath. She'll protect herself."

Kaleen whispered against his coat, "I can't find her. She's not answering."

"Did you check with her boyfriend? He might have better luck from his location."

She leaned back and looked at him, wiping her eyes, hope filling her. "Bridger, you're a genius."

Reaching for the Brazil Base, she sent, *"Ardense, are you there?"*

"Kaleen, is that you?"

"Can you reach Denefe?"

"Wait. What? I thought she was with you."

"A sidewinder took her. Try to reach her. Try as hard as you can."

The connection between them cut as if it had been via a comm link. Within a few seconds, he returned. *"I can't reach her either. You said it hit at your dig site?"*

"Yes, just a couple of minutes ago."

"All right. My team's already scrambling to try to find any residuals of the wormhole so we can map it. I'll notify Primary. You keep trying to contact her. I will too."

Kaleen, still pulled tight against Bridger's coat, nodded as if Ardense could see her. *"I will. Let me know right away if you find anything."*

68

"Absolutely." Then he was gone.

Her mind was empty of anyone else's thoughts. Even the comforting, constant, natural link between her and her twin was gone. She'd never felt so alone.

The sobs she'd quelled before swamped her as her heart broke. She crumpled to the frozen snow.

Denefe was missing. She might be dead.

Chapter 15
Sidewinder Justice

Denefe lay where the sidewinder had dropped her, afraid to hope that it was gone. Maybe there was just a lull, like the eye in a storm? There were no rift spiders. It *had* to be over. She slowly moved her hands away from her face, gasping in pain when her glove accidentally brushed against the part of her brow that had been uncovered. She'd have to seek medical attention, no doubt about that. She was sure some kind of damage had to have happened to her intestines too. First, though, she had to figure out where she was, and when.

Carefully, she raised her head and moved to sit from her open, prone position. Putting pressure on her intestines was pure agony, and she leaned back, propping herself up with her hands. Damage, indeed.

Where and when was she? Looking in the three directions, she saw only sand, nothing else. She turned to her side, groaning, and looked behind her. More sand. A desert. Great. Now what? She'd die out there without shelter or water. She already felt dehydrated from the sidewinder.

Now that she knew where she was, she wasn't sure she cared about the when.

She reached out telepathically for Kaleen, but couldn't find her. Kaleen might also have been snatched by the sidewinder and flung somewhere else, or was dead. Or, Denefe amended, there probably wasn't any regular rift opening nearby in the middle of the desert.

Her brow stung as sweat beaded on it. She looked at the sun directly overhead. That would be no help as a compass right now. The fierceness of its heat made her skin burn even more, and she dropped her face. Tugging her hood closer, she considered her options.

She could lie there, overheat, and die. She could struggle to take off her winter clothes and die more comfortably. She could stand and try to see from a higher vantage point what else lay out there, not that she really thought anything did. Or she could do a combination of all three. Actually, she probably would.

There was nothing for her to do but get up, and get on with her plans of dying. With a sigh, she gritted her teeth and shoved off the ground with her hand, bringing one knee in underneath her. The spear of pain that lanced through her gut almost caused her to abandon her plan. She collapsed to one side, sucking in deep breaths through pursed lips, trying to get her insides to stop shaking.

The tremors didn't stop, but instead crept further and further outward into her arms and legs. Her body chilled inside her coat. Shock! Whether she wanted to or not, now she had to get up. No way was she going to die from shock. No way. It would ruin the experience of dying from the heat of the desert.

She had to get up fast or she wouldn't do it at all. Rather like tearing a bandage off quickly. Again, she gritted her teeth and shoved off the ground with her hand. With a growling roar, she pushed her knees beneath her and then popped to her feet. Immediately, she doubled over from the spasms in her intestines, almost dropping to her knees again. If she went down this time, she'd never try to get up again. Feeling herself sway, she took one staggering step forward, and then another. After seven steps, she stopped.

Her body was still shaking uncontrollably, but at least it hadn't gotten worse. Now the question was— which was warmer? With or without the coat? She remembered from her school lessons that the Bedouins wore layers and layers of long robes to keep cool. Obediently, she fumbled with the coat fasteners at her throat. It seemed forever, but she managed to undo the top half. She took a deep breath and eased herself straight, moaning and biting her lip against the pain.

While she undid the rest of her coat, she looked around. Why waste the upright time? Still, only sand greeted her gaze on the three sides. On the fourth, so small she almost missed it, she saw a black speck in the distance. Was it really there? Or was it merely a mirage? Did it matter? She had to keep moving or die from shock. She might as well move in that direction as any.

She began her long, shaky journey. Each jarring step ricocheted up into her abdomen. As she walked, she experimented with different positions, straightening or leaning more and more forward, to see which cushioned her injuries the most. Finally, she settled on a forward leaning limp. The heat bore down on her, and she was thankful she still had her coat to protect her burned skin from the painful punishment of the sun. Her stomach settled into a numbing ache. Periodically, she stopped and checked her black-spot destination in the sand. Though it didn't seem to get any closer, at least it didn't move around, no matter which direction she looked.

That comforted her. It wasn't a mirage.

Starry kept plaguing her thoughts. She'd be willing to bet he'd gone through what she had. Only without the heavy protective clothing, he'd burned to a crisp. Even without the microchip injuring him like that, he'd never really stood a chance at surviving. He'd have fallen into shock and never come out, freezing to death.

Eventually, she warmed, and her shaking petered off. She should dig into the sand like the Bedouins and sleep off the rest of the heated day. Still, she plodded on until, at last, her weariness won out. When she checked the sun's position, it seemed it hadn't moved at all. It was pointless trying. It really was. She was just prolonging the agony of death, but she just couldn't give up.

Easing down to her knees, she dug into the desert floor. It wasn't easy. The scooping hurt her stomach, and she wasn't able to move the sand far from the hole. For every scoop she pulled out, almost a full one-third fell back in. Eventually, she gave up and moved into the hole anyway, turning sideways into a fetal position. It was really no more than just a depression, but still, it was something. She arranged her coat, careful to make sure it was tucked over her skin. Worming a free hand out from under, she scraped sand back on top of her. Every bit of insulation from the sun would help. Now, if the bugs and critters would just stay away.

The heat was suffocating underneath the coat, but it was better than being out in the sun. Denefe pulled the hood back from her face to let some fresh air in so she could breathe. When it got so hot she couldn't stand it anymore, she decided to move on. Perhaps, if she took these mini-breaks throughout her journey, she just might make it to the black speck.

Rising was, if anything, more painful than the last time. Besides her twisted intestines crying in pain, her stiff muscles added their own complaints. Eventually, though, she won out and began on her course again.

Each time she stopped and holed up, she was more exhausted and was willing to put up with more heat in her coat cocoon. It was physically harder to get up again. Finally, she sank to the ground, not caring that she didn't dig a hole or that she didn't pull her coat over her to protect her from the sun. She was done.

As blackness creeped into her vision, she once again thought of Starry. She wasn't much different from him, after all. She could almost hear Kaleen's voice in her mind, calling for her.

Chapter 16
Rescued

Torenz piloted the skimmer, coaxing the sand-choked engine across the endless dunes that more resembled the waves of a mighty ocean than dry land. He'd never gone out that far before, but he had no choice now. Stopping next to the still form of Denefe, he stared down at her. The hood of her heavy parka had fallen back, exposing snow-white locks.

He smiled. He'd often wondered what she and Kaleen looked like. His heart thundered in time with his thoughts—Denefe was there! Denefe was there!

He frowned and hopped out of the dust-covered skimmer. Denefe hadn't moved. She was too still. He heard nothing in her mind, but he wouldn't unless she actively thought something. Was she still alive?

Squatting beside her, he pushed his fingertips against her carotid artery in her neck. Her pulse was weak, but it was there.

Her weight surprised him as he lifted her and gently placed her into the grimy passenger's side of the skimmer. For someone so little, she had a lot of muscle.

Piloting back to the base over the waves of sand, he considered how to tell his boss that Denefe had appeared at his front door.

What about Kaleen? Someone needed to tell her Denefe was all right.

It couldn't be him, though.

He didn't exist.

Chapter 17
Cease and Desist

Kaleen stood on the platform at the GlobeX Siberian Telepathic Hub. She hated being there, hated the bad taste in her mouth every time she thought about how she'd worked there, hated the heavy crease in every employee's forehead, but mostly hated the weight of the politics of the place.

Yet right now, with Denefe missing, there was nowhere else she'd rather be. This place gave her the best shot at finding her twin.

Bridger leaned against the wall, as close to the rift as he was allowed, watching the silver swirls and eddies. The rest of the world could disappear and Kaleen didn't think he'd notice. He'd been good to her, immediately driving her there, not letting her pilot the shuttle or make the trip herself.

Rubbing her temple at the harsh ache building there, she tried not to let the panic enter her voice when she spoke to the base's chief engineer. "Tell me you caught the sidewinder that hit our dig."

The man who answered used to date her. He kept sneaking scowls at Bridger. "We definitely caught it. We're just having trouble accessing the data. Brazil Base may be having more luck with the stream we sent them."

She reached for Ardense with her mind. *:We're having difficulty up here. They say they can't access the info."*

"Here too. We're locked out. Although, Mik thinks he has a way around."

At that moment, the comm channel locked and then shut down.

Kaleen took an involuntary step forward, whispering, "No. Please, no."

After two minutes of hearing nothing but the rapid breathing and typing of the chief engineer, the channel came back on. Immediately, everyone got busy with their programs.

It was Ardense who gave Kaleen the news she dreaded, yet already knew in her heart. *"It's gone. Every bit of the data has been stripped from the stream. What about your end?"*

She eyed the frowns and confused faces of those around her. *"Probably. They're still checking."*

Now they'd never find Denefe. She pinched her lips tight, determined not to let the sobs take over again. She locked gazes with Bridger, and he crossed the platform to stand close beside her.

Ardense spoke again. *"Listen, it's a good sign. Denefe has to be alive."*

Kaleen held her breath and placed her hand on Bridger's chest, ignoring the threatening glare of the chief engineer. Her heart grasped at the thin straw of hope. *"How do you figure that?"*

"If she was dead, they would have told us so we'd stop looking. Instead, they stripped the data and didn't

78

say a word."

Slowly, she calmed. It made sense.

Ardense continued. *"She must have landed near some place restricted. Like—"*

"Primary. She landed near Primary." Kaleen sat at an empty station and opened a comm link. The moment the receptionist at GlobeX Primary Hub answered, his mouth rounded to an "O" and he put her on hold. She hadn't even had time to give her name. It seemed they'd been expecting her call.

Within seconds, she found herself facing Maurice Cardenza. His chiseled face looked gaunter and worn than usual. The dark bags that normally underscored his eyes were positively charcoal.

He began immediately. "If you call anyone else here, they'll just reroute you to me, so don't bother hanging up."

"You stole our data."

He gave a thin smile. "*Our* data was brought here so we could put our very best people on it and find answers quickly."

"Mik at Brazil Base is one of the best."

He cleared his throat. "Actually, no. We don't send the best out. They're all right here." He jammed his index finger straight down on the desk for emphasis.

Kaleen could almost feel steam rolling from her ears at his arrogance. She'd never liked him, but now she absolutely hated him. Before she could stop herself, she blurted, "Do you have Denefe? We know the sidewinder probably landed near someplace restricted." She hadn't planned on letting anyone at GlobeX know what they'd figured out, but her anger had gotten the better of her and there it was.

He sighed, crossed his fingers, and leaned into the camera. "The data suggests she made it through the sidewinder alive, but she's not here. However, I

79

understand your worries. I have some concerns as well. I'll send my people into every room of the complex for a visual search. The surrounding area too. I promise, we'll find out what happened to your sister."

Kaleen sat back as the screen went black. For all her dislike of Maurice Cardenza, he seemed to be genuinely sincere in his effort to help. He would find Denefe. She was alive.

Or had been when she was dumped by the sidewinder.

Chapter 18
Where is Here?

Slowly, Denefe awoke from a dreamless state. She was in a structure of some kind. Frowning, she concentrated on what she could remember. It was only one thing—the desert. So, how'd she get there? Where was here? Assuming it was the same sidewinder that snatched Starry, was she in Egypt? Had it reversed itself, not in time—the furnishings of the room were modern—but in location? She'd never heard of one doing that before, but so little was known about them.

A door opened, bringing with it indistinct sounds of voices laughing and talking. A dark-haired woman approached, holding an ornate silver tray bearing fruits and an assortment of cooked dishes. The woman was medium build, but her hands were as big as, if not bigger than, a relatively large-sized man's.

Denefe waved her away. Food was the last thing she wanted. Her insides felt raw and bruised as if she'd been run over by a military tank.

Instead of leaving, the woman set the tray on a little

nightstand and lowered herself to the edge of the bed. "You need to eat. It will aid the healing process. The questions you have must wait until you are better." Her voice was soft as honey and her face beneath thick brown hair looked to be olive-toned in the darkened room. "My name is Jileah, and I'm going to help you sit up now."

She slid a large hand behind Denefe's shoulder and, with the other, took hold of her opposite elbow. Slowly, Denefe rose to a sitting position. By the time she'd leaned back on the prepared pillows, she was drenched in sweat and her insides quivered like a dying fish.

Jileah settled the tray on the bed and then lifted an empty spoon. "Can you eat, or do you think you might need some help?"

Denefe shook her head and reached for the spoon. She didn't think she could trust her voice to speak.

"Good. I'll check back in a little bit." With that, Jileah stood and left, closing the door behind her.

Alone again, Denefe looked around the room. The walls were painted warm ochre. At the far wall squatted a dresser with a metronome on top. Above hung a photograph of her parents. It was a favorite of hers. Her parents had been married for seven years and thought they'd never be able to have children. The picture had been taken the day her mother had found out she was pregnant. She was flushed with a shy smile, but her father grinned like the Cheshire cat. If a person looked closely enough, the glint of tears could be seen in her parents' eyes.

The frame was different and the photo was larger, but the fact that it was there meant she was at GlobeX Primary. Denefe sighed and closed her eyes. Home. Right now, it was the most wonderful-sounding word in the world.

The fruit on her tray was an assortment of fresh

peaches, kiwi, and figs. Fresh fruit from all over the globe meant it had to be shipped in. That meant money. Definitely, GlobeX. There was a brothy rice soup, thinly sliced meat in gravy, and mixed mashed vegetables.

She took a few bites of everything and finished with the caramel-flavored drink. Settling her head back on the pillow, she tried to remember how she came to be there, but nothing came to her, except sleep. Just before she gave in, she started to full wakefulness. She needed to contact her twin.

"Kaleen."

"Denefe! I'm so glad to hear you. Are you all right?" Her thought-voice ran together almost as one word. It came across crystal clear and exceedingly loud.

"How long have I been missing?"

"Three days. Are you okay?"

Denefe blinked. *"I've been unconscious for three days?"*

"Unconscious? Are. You. Okay?"

"Yes. I. Think. So."

"Don't get snippy with me. You're the one who disappeared."

Denefe had no rejoinder for that, but it sobered her. *"Yeah. I'm sorry."*

"So what happened?"

"Got sucked up in a sidewinder that tried to rip me in half. Landed in a desert in the middle of the day with no shelter in sight. Passed out, I guess, and woke up here. That's all I know."

"Where's 'here'?"

"I'm at GlobeX Primary."

"No, I checked already. You're not there."

Denefe frowned. *"Not there? Then where am I?"*

"I don't know. You'll have to find out on your end. We're all out of ideas."

"GlobeX doesn't know?"

83

"They say they don't, but you know them."

"Well, I think I'm at a GlobeX hub somewhere, even if it isn't Primary."

"That gives us something to pursue. Have you spoken to Ardense yet? He's furious because no one has told us anything."

"No doubt. I'll talk to him right away."

"I'll go so you can do that now. I'm glad you're okay, and don't worry, we'll figure out where you are."

"I don't worry. That's your department."

"Ha ha. I'll talk to you soon."

Then she was gone. A well of loneliness swelled within Denefe. She stretched her mind for her boyfriend.

"Ardense, are you there?"

His voice answered immediately. Worry and fear laced through his words. *"Where are you?"*

"What? No pleasantries? No words of endearment?"

"Denefe!"

She smiled. He was worried about her.

"I don't know where I am, but it's somewhere within the GlobeX fiefdom. Kaleen and I just can't figure out which hub." Denefe cringed as she realized her error. He was too smart to not notice it, but she held on to a small hope, anyway.

He paused and then asked, *"Kaleen knew you were okay and didn't tell me?"* His telepathic voice left no doubt that she was in trouble. She hurried to placate him, wishing she could wrap her arms around him to reassure him.

"I just now spoke to her. It's the first time since the sidewinder took me."

Disbelief dripped from his words. *"You called her first."*

"You're mad at GlobeX. Don't take it out on me."

Ardense was silent for so long, Denefe decided to

84

leave the conversation. Before she could say anything, he spoke again. *"I'm sorry. I've just been out of my mind worrying about you. Those idiots, Cardenza and Hallen, won't tell me a thing or let me help. Are you sure you're okay?"*

"Yeah, pretty much. I just gotta figure out where I am."

"Be careful and let me know right away. Love you."

"Yep. Talk to you later."

Long after Ardense left the conversation, Denefe lay awake turning the events over and over again. She was injured, but supposedly healing. No one knew where she was located. She, yet again, couldn't tell her boyfriend, who loved her and whom she loved, that she loved him. Finally, with no answers, she fell asleep, dreaming of sand and spiders.

Chapter 19
Who Are You?

When Denefe next opened her eyes, she gingerly tested the range of her movements and the pain associated with them. She could twist in either direction a little and bend her torso a small amount. Deciding she could sit up, if she moved slowly, Denefe carefully raised her upper body. Reaching blindly behind her, she propped up her pillow. Step one accomplished.

Now for step two.

Inch-by-inch, she bent her knees, keeping her feet flat on the bed. She pushed. Instantly, a knife-cut of agony sliced through her gut. Gasping, she froze. When the pain didn't leave, she lowered her legs again and lay back, not bothering to flatten her pillow. She breathed deeply through pursed lips, trying to calm the quiver that now drove her stomach.

Jileah rushed in. "What happened?"

Denefe gave a wan smile. "Too soon to sit up on my own, I guess." Her voice came out as a croak.

"I'll help you." As before, Jileah cradled Denefe's upper back in her strangely massive hands and pulled her into a sitting position.

"How did you know I needed help? Are you a telepath or empath?"

Her nurse raised her brows. "Me? No, I'm not, but I..." Her brow furrowed. "I was told by our resident telepath here that you were in trouble." She turned and whisked out the door.

Denefe frowned. She'd wanted to ask that woman questions, but she'd been dodged again. Well, when direct questions wouldn't work, there was another way a telepath could get information. Most people couldn't control automatic responses, no matter how hard they tried.

She called after her nurse, "Thank you for bringing me to the southern GlobeX hub."

The trick worked. A short phrase appeared in the retreating woman's mind, correcting Denefe's error— *"Definitive Headquarters."*

Jileah was almost out of earshot now. There was time for only one more question. "You rescued me from the Egyptian Desert?"

"Gobi."

Denefe turned that latest information over in her mind. So, the sidewinder hadn't reversed itself, after all. She'd never heard of anything GlobeX had in the Gobi Desert. It had to be GlobeX or Jileah would have corrected that in her mind as well. What was Definitive Headquarters?

She sighed and reached for her drink. It was then that she realized she was no longer alone.

Denefe's heart lurched. The man standing at the door looked enough like Kaleen to be identical—same white hair, same pointed chin, same short and slim frame. No, she thought, looking at his skintight pants and the muscles defined there. Kaleen was petite. She didn't have muscles like that. Denefe, herself, did. That man could be her twin.

He walked into the room, watching her. "It's amusing to see the way your mind works. So quick and agile. Not like Kaleen's. It's actually more like mine." He sat beside Denefe on the edge of the bed.

A chill ran through her. He knew them. She asked, "Who are you?"

Instead of answering the direct question, he turned his head and nodded at the portrait above the dresser. "What do you remember of them? I mean, actually remember, not what you've been told."

"They were killed in a plane wreck when Kaleen and I were babies. So, not much." She didn't want to talk about her parents. She wanted to talk about him. She repeated, "Who are you?"

"What *do* you remember?"

All right. She'd play his game. "I remember hands. Hers were strong and fine. His were big and gentle. I remember her perfume too."

He nodded. "White Oleander. Is that all?"

"Why?"

"What if I told you they didn't die that day? That the accident was staged and they lived for another twelve years before they actually died from quite a different accident. Would you hate them?"

Denefe frowned. Her parents hadn't died in the plane accident? "Why didn't they contact us?"

"Because they couldn't." He paced the room. "They were brought here to do research for a level ten project."

"For GlobeX."

"Yes."

"What kind of work?"

"Nothing I can tell you about just yet."

Understanding leaped into Denefe. "So…you're my brother. You were born later, after they came here."

"Um, no. Not quite."

"You're a clone?"

"Definitely not." He shook his head vehemently.

"What then? Who are you?"

He stopped pacing and locked gazes with her. "My name is Torenz. I'm your triplet."

Denefe stared at him. Could they be? True, they looked similar, and he had the muscles to prove his athleticism like her. The part of their thought patterns being alike was sketchy proof at best. Really, triplets? Either that man was delusional or someone was trying to trick her. The third option, that it was true, was just too farfetched.

Chapter 20
Who Am I?

Denefe was at a loss for words. She stared at the lean, white-haired man in front of her. Could Torenz really be a triplet? It seemed wildly untrue. Yet he looked so similar to her and Kaleen. Inadvertently, her gaze flicked to the photo of her parents.

Torenz's thought-voice filled her mind. *"I assure you, it's true and I'm not delusional."*

Her bridled response was immediate as she snapped her gaze back to him. *"You're very rude to sit in my mind uninvited."*

"I've been doing it for quite a few years now. Just keeping tabs on the two of you. You're right, though. I'm sorry. You aren't much better, treating poor Jileah the way you did."

"It's different. She refused to tell me any information. Ergo, she was possibly a hostile force."

"Ah, good old GlobeX training." He paced again. "Tell me, did she actually refuse or did she promise to tell you later?"

Denefe shrugged. "Semantics."

"I see. So, by extension, you think I could be hostile?"

"Well, I'm pretty sure you're lying about being a triplet. Plus, you still haven't told me where or when I am." Denefe felt her face flush with heated anger. It didn't help that Torenz stopped, slack-jawed, and stared at her. She snapped, "What?"

He shook his head. "You're so like Dad." He smiled, sorrow pulling the corners of his eyes and mouth downward. "You're smack in the middle of the Gobi Desert, circa 322 BC. This installation is deep underground, where it's cool. We found you because I heard your thoughts in this time instead of the future where they usually belong. When you're well enough, we'll get our genomes tested and compared so I can prove I'm not lying." He turned to leave.

"I'm well enough now."

He stopped and faced her. "You're joking. You can't even sit up without help."

"You're right, but since I have you to help me, let's go."

"Now I know how Mom felt. She never could stand up to Dad. I'll be right back." He laughed and left.

Denefe had just set her drink back on the nightstand and contemplated how to get up when a small shuttle cart floated into the room, Torenz driving. He stopped four feet from the bed and dismounted.

"This will hurt a little, so it's important you concentrate on being limp like a wet rag. Let me do the work."

Denefe nodded, and he pulled back the covers. Sliding his hands under her knees and behind her shoulders, he carefully lifted her, stepped round the cart, and deposited her into the driver's seat. The whole procedure took less than a minute, but to Denefe, who

91

waited for the sharp lances of pain to appear, it seemed to take forever. She was pleased, therefore, when the ache wasn't as harsh as she'd expected.

"How far are we traveling?"

Torenz spun the cart on its layer of air to face the door. "Down the hall, left, right, through three intersections, left, and left."

"Got it." She took off, not waiting to see if he followed. The halls seemed to stretch longer and longer the closer they came to their destination, and she kept the cart at maximum speed the whole trip. By the time they arrived, Torenz, who had picked up a steady jog, was sweating.

Without comment, he opened the door to the lab. They were greeted by Jileah, who seemed not to have noticed or cared about Denefe's transgression against her.

Torenz said, "We'd like a DNA test, please, Jileah."

"Gladly. I just need a sample of each of your DNA. Saliva is the most non-invasive."

Jileah handed them each swabs and prepared two slides. After placing the saliva samples onto the glass plates, she slid them into flat depressions under the lens of a machine that looked remotely like a mechanical Mr. Magoo. Two images of striated bars appeared side-by-side on a large monitor on the wall. A blue light traced each bar, lingering in the striations. As the beam moved, a compatibility percentage continuously evaluated and recalculated until the light reached the end of the charts—ninety-eight percent.

Jileah looked from one to the other. "That's closer than blood relatives. You're nearly identical."

Stunned, Denefe's mind reeled. It was really true that Torenz was a triplet. Did that mean the rest of his story was true as well? Her parents hadn't died in the wreck. Had they really, instead, chosen to abandon two of their children and gone to live in the past with their son?

It felt as if the life had been squeezed out of her and her heart was nothing but an aching, bottomless pit. Her parents had rejected her and Kaleen. Whirling her cart on its pad of air, she launched it out the open door and down the first hall she came to. Without signs, there was no way Denefe could tell where she was going. It wasn't as though she cared. Anywhere was fine as long as it was fast and far. She chose new corridors as whim took her. Every open stretch, she pushed the cart to high speed, startling not a few people. She imagined Torenz was somewhere behind her. Not that she cared about that either.

How could her parents just abandon her and Kaleen? Why weren't they good enough to keep?

Taking a turn too fast, her cart lurched to the left, banking hard and almost tumbling. Once it settled upright again, it had a peculiar bump as it rode, almost as if traveling over logs. Lost and emotionally spent, she let her vehicle slow to a stop.

After Torenz eventually found her, she asked, her voice no louder than a whisper, "Why?"

"Let's get you back to bed first. Then we'll sit and talk about it all."

Resentment filled her. Watching him as she navigated her cart behind him, she resented the straightness of his back, the muscular curve of his shoulders, the easy gait that was so much like hers.

Once they reached her room, she waited in silence while he scooped her out of the cart and settled her on the bed. Before he could speak, she said, "I'd rather not talk right now. Please leave."

Torenz opened his mouth as if to say something, but after a couple of seconds, he snapped it shut and nodded. He started to leave, but walked to the dresser, picked up the metronome seated there, and brought it to her nightstand. He walked out the door, cart in tow.

Denefe stared at her parents' photo, a riot of emotions playing within her. The wreck that supposedly had killed them was one of the worst in aeronautical history. The new Intercontinental Rocket Plane, Flight 610R, was supposed to have left Dulles International at 11:05 in the morning and arrive in Geneva after a seventy-five-minute flight. That had been the schedule. In truth, Flight 610R never even made it off the ground. A small twenty-passenger commuter plane had taxied onto the wrong runway. As the giant rocket plane had roared to takeoff speed, the commuter pilot had tried desperately to navigate far enough to the side for safe passage. The departing plane's massive wing, where the fuel was stored, had struck the smaller craft midsection and they both had erupted into a ball of flames. All passengers from the commuter had died instantly. Only seventeen of the 557 aboard 610R had survived. Her parents had been among the listed dead.

She and Kaleen had only gotten information about the wreck second-hand. They'd been far too young to remember anything, except that their parents' hands had never returned to hold them again. She was glad they hadn't died in the wreck. Glad they'd lived another twelve years. Now she hated them. How could they have abandoned their two daughters? How was she going to tell Kaleen?

Unable to stand the sight of her parents anymore, she closed her eyes. She'd rather tear the photo off the wall and shatter it into a million shards, but that would wait until another day when she could walk.

She tried to turn her thoughts to her predicament and how best to get home, but, like a yo-yo, her mind kept returning to her parents' deception.

Finally, with a growl, she opened her eyes and

reached for the wooden metronome Torenz had placed on the nightstand. She'd always admired the pyramidal shape and feel of the smoothly-grained wood, but this one was stunning beyond compare. It was made with what looked to be olive wood, the grain striations giving it a marbled look. She set the weight to medium height. After winding it, she set it back onto the nightstand and started it up. The deep, mellow toc-toc-toc of the swinging weight against the olive wood distracted her from her thoughts.

It took some time for the easy rhythm to smooth the harsh edges of her emotions. Even longer before she felt the first stirrings of calm. Through it all, she kept her eyes closed. Still, she wasn't entirely oblivious to her environment. At one point, Jileah came in with food and left it sitting beside the metronome. Sometime later, she returned, presumably to collect the dishes, and then left. The tray stayed behind. Denefe could still smell the meat sauce. At another point, someone stood at her door for a long time before leaving. Denefe thought it might be Torenz, not because he said or did anything, but because it would be something Kaleen would do.

On the rare occasion she and Kaleen fought, her twin always got over her anger quickly. Denefe, on the other hand, harbored hers close like a lover, letting it eat through her and consume her until all combustible thoughts were burned away. It took days.

Chapter 21
The Plan

Torenz lay back on his bed, counting the cracks in the ceiling, his fingers laced behind his head, trying to nap, but he was far too wound up to do that. He'd been that way since he'd found his sister in the desert four days ago. Distraction helped him doze, but he always woke up within a few hours. He needed sleep, however, it was proving to be an elusive friend.

In person, Denefe was much different than her thoughts. For one, she was testier, but he was used to that in Mom. It didn't bother him much. His sister had proven she was fair. He'd seen that in how she'd accepted the results of the DNA tests. Her upset hadn't been because of the relationship. It had been because of their parents' apparent lie.

In her thoughts, Denefe was vocal and confident, almost aggressive. There, in person, she was quiet. He'd seen her as unsure. Of course that most probably had something to do with circumstances that made her show a different side of herself. Multifaceted was what she was. Like him.

He'd been given orders regarding her. She was not allowed to investigate the facility alone. She was not to be told anything about the anomaly. Nor was she allowed near it. There would be no discussion of his mission, either.

Under no circumstances was she allowed to leave. Ever.

Chapter 22
Back to Training

Each time the metronome's hollow toc-toc-toc slowed to a stop, Denefe rewound it. It had been some time since she'd trained with one, and when she calmed enough, she began the exercises she'd been taught as a small child.

Toc-toc-toc. She let the sound of the instrument pull her deep into herself and clear her thoughts away. When she was a child, she would swing back and forth in time with the soothing rhythm. The teachers at the GlobeX fosterage initially checked her for autism, but found none. They were just motions, nothing more. They amused the teachers so much, they even encouraged it. Somehow, someone up the chain of command got wind and issued the order to stop the movements. Denefe found her once-cute mannerisms suddenly worthy of chastisement. It was one of the loneliest days of her childhood. It was also the day she learned the true meaning of being a telepath. Kaleen had sent a quiet message to Denefe's mind. *"I'm here."*

From that moment on, she and Kaleen bonded stronger than any other pair in the fosterage. Not a day went by that they weren't constantly in touch telepathically.

Toc-toc-toc. She left all thoughts about her past and let the metronome take them. The silence and clarity within her allowed her to relax. Her breathing slowed, and she felt her recent frown smooth away.

Moving easily into the second part of her childhood training, she pictured her mind as a flower and slowly opened it to the cacophony of thought-voices around her. Most people were on constant broadcast.

"...time to eat? I'm starved."

"...to the root of the fifteenth..."

"...isn't what she said..."

They all overlapped each other, and it took a few minutes, but she eventually identified eighteen separate voices. There weren't as many as she'd thought. The facility must be small. Or some must be on alternate shifts.

Slowly she closed the "petals" of the flower, blocking the voices one by one until there were none. She held the silence in her mind, listening to the lack of constant murmur that she filtered through each day. After a few moments, she began the exercise again. Each time she reached the end of the cycle and stopped to listen to the silence, she stretched the time longer. She usually repeated the cycle eight to ten times before she was finished.

After the tenth time, the question of how she was going to tell Kaleen about Torenz came unbidden to her mind. She firmly pushed it away and concentrated on listening to the quiet and the toc-toc-toc.

At once, another thought arose—Torenz had eavesdropped on her thoughts before. Was he listening now?

Denefe reached for the flower image again, opening it all the way and then closing one petal at a time. She did that twice more. The last time, as she closed the petals, she was careful to not shut out her link with Torenz.

Focusing on the hollow rhythm of her metronome, she waited in silence for a few minutes. She broadcast, *"I wonder what time of day it is? It must be afternoon."*

Immediately, Torenz's mind corrected, *"Evening."*

Pretending she hadn't heard him, she thought to herself, *"I should talk to Kaleen again. Maybe after a nap. I'm awfully tired."*

She lay down, closed her eyes, and let herself drown in the toc-toc-toc of her metronome, waiting and forcing herself to breathe slow and deep. It took what seemed like hours, but in all probability was only fifteen minutes before Torenz's thoughts became wrapped up in who won a chess tournament.

She sat up and stared at her parents in the photo. They stared back, mocking her.

"Kaleen."

"Hello, sister mine. Feeling better?" Kaleen's voice was alarmingly loud and clear.

"Better, yes. Do you remember that blue dress we always fought over as children?" That was their code that one or both of them may be monitored telepathically. They'd invented it when in fosterage and it had served them well over the years. It was an elaborate code that no one had ever been able to crack. It required them both to respond fast without thinking. There had been no blue dress.

Without hesitation, Kaleen answered, *"I absolutely do."*

"I still maintain it was mine." The only important word in that sentence was "mine." It meant she was starting the coded message. The second word in the next

100

passage was the code word. The question at the end indicated that passage was over. *"The pin was gorgeous. Do you remember it?"*

How Kaleen answered wasn't important, only that she didn't ask for a repeat. Her job was to make Denefe's sometimes oddly forced sentences sound normal. *"I certainly do!"*

"The hole it tore in the dress was sad, though. I forget who did that, do you know?"

"I think it was Kathlet. She wanted the pin."

"Her metronome was damaged too. Or was it?"

"I think you're right."

"Well, once she found she couldn't have the pin, she quit being friends with me. Was she still yours?" The message was over. Pin. Hole. Metronome. Once. Denefe had used the word "quit" to tell her sister the message was over.

"No, she quit me too." Kaleen also used "quit." She had no message of her own.

They chatted about nothing consequential for a few minutes before Denefe said, *"I'm tired and going to nap now. I'll talk to you tomorrow."*

"Be careful and get better. A nap sounds like just the ticket." Kaleen couldn't keep worry from lacing through her thoughts. She left.

Denefe reached for her dinner on her nightstand. It was cold, of course, but it was still tasty and she didn't have to work hard to choke it down. While she ate, she stared at the portrait on the wall. Perhaps she wouldn't destroy it. Her parents, though dead, could be useful, after all.

She checked on Torenz, who was still obsessing over chess. He'd been listening in on her thoughts twice now. That she knew. He'd told her that he'd found her because her thoughts were there instead of in the future "as they usually were." That meant he'd been listening for a long time. Why? Was it just a brother's curiosity?

No matter the reason, it didn't bode well as far as trust was concerned. She'd bet money that no matter how much he swore he'd never do it again, she'd find him inside her mind, spying. Now, because of his actions, she was going to have to take care with what she let herself think. She was going to have to lie and spy into his mind occasionally.

It filled her with distaste, and she returned her half-empty tray to the nightstand. She hated this skulking around stuff. It was part of why she was so happy to be posted at Brazil Base in the middle of nowhere, far from politics. That was a sentimentality she shared with Kaleen.

Tomorrow, she would begin her investigation into her parents' disappearance. Why had they come to this place? What was "Definitive Headquarters"? Why were they hidden so deep in the desert? How was she going to get home? Most importantly, how was she going to tell Kaleen she had a brother?

She broke off her thoughts and checked on Torenz again. He'd changed topics, but not by much. Now he obsessed over some kind of game called Crimson King. Could she trust him? Trust what he'd told her?

It had been a while since she'd had to fly by the seat of her pants, without thinking first. Trust her instinct. Tomorrow would be the beginning of a whole new pattern for her...again. For now, there was nothing she could do.

Chapter 23
Up and About

Denefe awoke early on the fifth day from another dream about being chased by giant spiders the color of sand. For a moment, she lay in bed wondering which life was the real one—the spider-world or the one where she'd fallen through time into a desert only to discover everything she'd known was a lie.

Her dream had been so vivid and detailed. She went over it again in her mind, looking for hidden meaning but finding none. It seemed to be about nothing more than anxiety brought on by her frustrations and fears in that strange place.

She sat up, noting it was much easier than the day before. Testing her limbs in a full range of movements, she found the pain, while still there, had lessened considerably. With a grim smile, she carefully twisted to hang her legs over the side. She had something to do.

Placing her feet flat on the floor, Denefe eased herself into a standing position. It wasn't exactly comfortable. Perhaps she rushed things a bit and ought to go back to bed, but she wouldn't. Her anger at her parents, for their abandonment, was too strong. She was furious with Torenz too. He shouldn't be listening in her mind whenever he felt like it.

She took a tentative step and cringed at the sudden slice of agony across her abdomen, questioning her decision to walk, but she was an athlete and was used to pain and pushing through it. Denefe braced herself against the mattress and took another step and another. Her teeth were bared in defiance as she traveled the length of the bed.

Reaching the end, she hesitated only a brief second before stepping into the middle of the room, arms outstretched for balance like a tightrope walker. It took a millennia to cross to the dresser, but she made it. She slumped against the drawer faces and looked up at her parents' photo. "Did you see that? Kaleen's just as tough, but in different ways. You shouldn't have left us behind. We were worth your love and time."

Denefe reached up, removed the picture from the wall, and placed it face down on the dresser. She wasn't going to destroy it. Torenz might want it later. She didn't have to have it in her face, either.

"I hope your baby boy was worth it."

She turned and began her slow journey back to her bed. Halfway up the mattress, Torenz made his appearance. He glanced at her dresser, and said, "Redecorating, I see."

She didn't look at him. The smile was evident in his voice. "So glad you find this amusing." She let her sarcasm contaminate her words. One more step and then she could ease the weight off her shaking legs.

"Amusing? Nope. I'm just trying to lighten your mood." He walked into the room as she turned and prepared to relax on the bed.

Lowering, her abdominal muscles screamed with

pain at the half-sit point, so she let herself fall the rest of the way. It wasn't particularly graceful, but a whole lot less painful.

Torenz raised his eyebrows, but wisely said nothing about her lack of elegance. Instead, he asked, "So, can I stay, or am I still on a 'Please leave' notice?"

"I want my clothes, not these pajamas."

As if waiting for an answer to his question or worrying what to say to her request, he stared at her a moment. He crossed to the dresser and pulled out some clothes from the top drawer. Placing them beside her on the bed, he said, "Yours were destroyed. Besides, you don't need a parka here."

She reached for her clothes and he left the room, closing the door behind him.

Denefe picked up the smooth, sleeveless shirt first. If she could walk to the dresser, then she could dress herself. So what if it took her a little longer than usual. However, it took her so long Torenz knocked on the door, offering help, which she refused. By the time she finished, beads of sweat slid down her brow.

"I'm dressed," she called to the door.

Torenz entered, leading the shuttle cart. "I'd like to get breakfast sometime before supper tonight." He grinned.

In spite of the slow burn of anger within her, she smiled weakly. She was starving too.

It took almost no time to get to the tiny dining room. It boasted only four tables, each with six chairs. Her original estimation of eighteen people seemed to be correct. At that moment, only five of the chairs were filled. From the furtive glances cast in her direction, she could guess the topic of conversation.

Trying not to be conspicuous, she tucked her white hair behind her ears, wishing for a hat. She chose a diagonal table from the group of three, across from the pair playing chess, limiting the ease of which she could be studied.

Torenz emerged from the kitchen with two plates and joined her. While they ate, he told her about the facility.

"The anomaly here was the first one mapped. When the most sophisticated telecom devices all failed, people were sent through. They died and no one knew the reason. The idea was hit upon to use a telepath. The first one died without anyone the wiser as to why."

"Because it's only telepath to telepath through the rifts. Links with normal people won't hold." She pointed her spoon at him. It amused her that he called it by the scientific term—anomaly. It made sense, since he'd been surrounded by scientists pretty much all his life.

He nodded. "The second time, the telepaths were ready. The first one arrived, and choked on sand. He tried to return but couldn't. That's when they discovered it was a one-way trip."

"One way? Wait. What? Am I trapped here?" Denefe's mind skittered sideways. Never go home again, to never see Kaleen or Ardense again? No. It couldn't be true. She wouldn't believe it. There had to be a way. There was always a way.

Torenz held up his hand, forestalling any more questions. It did little to calm the chaos in her mind, though. He said, "Immediately, his partner called for oxygen and sent it and supplies through with a three-man digging team. Within a few hours, they'd dug a tent-sized compartment."

"They kept digging and building and shipping over equipment ever since."

"Yes. As you can imagine, GlobeX was eager to begin studying the anomaly from this side. When they did, they discovered there were more. Each a long tunnel through space and time, sometimes their walls missing

106

each other by mere centimeters."

"Sidewinders?"

"That's what happens when the tunnels actually *do* touch. See, they're always moving, some more than others. It's just the two ends that are fixed. When they touch, they don't just cross one into the other, they often shoot out arms and legs to other locations. Most times, they're only temporary. Occasionally, they stabilize and we get multiple points from the same hub."

"Brazil Base."

"And the Siberian hub, where Kaleen is stationed. Or was, until she decided on the archaeology trip."

Denefe bit her lip. Her brother seemed to know a lot about her and Kaleen's lives. He had been listening to them *a lot*. She asked, "So, if the hubs are multiple tunnels, connected, then how are we able to go to the jump we want and not randomly land at one of the other points?" She'd never before cared to know about the workings of the rifts. It seemed important now, though.

"That's actually easier than you think. We're injected with a computer chip." Torenz tapped his temple.

The hair on the back of Denefe's neck bristled. In her mind, she again saw Starry's damaged head and Bridger pointing to where the chip had been lodged. "We all have one?"

"Every one of us. When the primary CAE sets the destination code into the computer, a message is sent to our chip, which then emits a sonic pitch that coincides with the pitch of the tunnel we want to travel. Dad came up with that one."

"Why were our parents here?"

"They were that first team. The ones I told you about. Dad came through first, was choking so Mom sent oxygen and diggers to him."

Denefe once again felt her world turn upside down.

107

Yet another lie. She'd always been told that the telepathic ability had skipped generations, that her parents hadn't been telepaths.

Chapter 24
Toc-toc-toc

Back in her tent at the dig, Kaleen rummaged through Denefe's bags until she found the small green metronome. It looked like hers and her sister's, but the thing was oddly weighted as she turned it over and over in her hands.

Pin, hole, metronome, once, Denefe had said.

Holding it close, she inspected its smooth wooden sides, but saw no pin hole of any kind. Furthermore, she saw no telltale scar that made it Denefe's. The damage had happened when they'd been rough-housing as children. They'd bumped a desk and sent the metronome crashing to the floor, leaving a long scratch in its back.

So, if it wasn't her sister's, whose was it? Why did Denefe have it?

Kaleen peered closely at the gold GlobeX emblem on the front.

She didn't see anything there either, but as she ran her thumb around the edge, her nail caught in the dark shadow of the outside circle. Pulling the metronome even closer, she saw the tiny pinhole. Clever. If she hadn't known to look for it, she wouldn't have seen it.

She narrowed her eyes at the archeological marker she'd set nearby to use as a pin. The stem was too wide for the hole. She rose from her curled position on the floor of the tent, stepped across Denefe's bags to her jewelry box, and fetched an earring that had been her mother's. After removing the clip on the back, she pushed the point of the post into the hole. Nothing happened.

Turning the metronome over and over again, she finally discovered a tiny hole hidden in the wood grain of the base. She pressed the earring into it, and immediately a recorded voice began speaking in some foreign language.

With a heavy frown, Kaleen considered what to do. Denefe's message had been explicit in pushing the pin once. She didn't dare tamper with it again.

She grabbed a heavy towel from Denefe's bag and wrapped it tightly around the still-speaking metronome. Donning her parka, she bolted out the door for Bridger's lab.

If he didn't understand what the recording was saying, he probably knew someone who did.

Chapter 25
Whys and Wherefores

Denefe's mind was still reeling after breakfast with Torenz. When he decided on an impromptu tour of the facility, she half-mindedly agreed. Her brother chattered on, but she heard nothing he said. She didn't believe what he'd said about the one-way-ness of the rift. There had to be a way. She pushed it aside for later.

The thing that occupied her now was that her parents hadn't died in the rocket plane wreck. They'd lived on, there, in this underground lab. While abandoning two baby girls, they'd kept the boy. They'd worked for GlobeX. They were telepaths. They were complete strangers and nothing of what she'd been told. She'd grown up knowing them in a certain way, accustomed to the feel of being an orphan. This upside-down feeling of not really knowing them swamped her.

Torenz stopped outside a door, one of a dozen that looked the same. "This was Mom and Dad's quarters. Well, mine too. I still live here." Torenz made as to move on, but Denefe piloted the shuttle car closer to the door.

"Do you still have their things? May I see?"

He hesitated, a play of emotions crossing his face. He shrugged and then opened the door.

The rooms were cozy with two bedrooms off a main family area. She parked her shuttle car and gingerly worked to her feet. It didn't hurt as much as the early morning walk had, but it was enough to make her catch her breath a few times.

Torenz pointed to the smaller of the two bedrooms. "I moved their stuff in there so I could have the bigger room."

Angling the trajectory of her shuffle-creep toward the indicated room, she found herself nodding. She would have changed rooms too. "I think most people would do that."

"Yeah, well, it made me feel pretty guilty for a long time."

Denefe paused her slow walk and met his gaze. There was an uncertain quality to the way he stood, hunched with hands in his pockets. He wanted her understanding. Her approval. Turning back to her target destination, she said, "These people aren't who I was told my parents were, but I can't see any parent not wanting the best for their...son. That includes bigger bedrooms...I guess."

This last she said more to herself as confusion ran her over. Again, she wondered about these people called her mother and father. Real parents didn't just abandon their children. Maybe she'd find some answers there.

She glanced quickly at her brother, but he seemed content with the acceptance she'd given. Had he even noticed her hesitation?

Stopping at the door, she viewed the room and its contents. A small bed sat in the corner. Probably Torenz's old one. Piles of children's toys and clothes rested on it along with a separate pile for items obviously made by a child. Gifts to Mommy and Daddy?

She was suddenly quite sick of feeling sorry for herself. Her parents had had a reason for what they'd done. She just needed to figure it out. Depending on what she found, it could go a long way toward forgiveness.

Torenz watched from the door as Denefe slowly crossed the room. The dresser top was crammed with her parents' personal items, including a pocket watch, matching hair brush set, plain barrettes, hair bands, and several pairs of glasses. The drawers were stuffed with clothes, ancient physics books, scientific journals, and electronic tablets.

She picked up a copy of *Physics, Then and Now*. "What's with all the hard copies?"

"Dad had macular degeneration. As time went on, it became more and more difficult for him to read the electronic tablets. Bringing an eye surgeon here on a one-way ticket wasn't a possibility."

There was that phrase again—one-way. She tightened her mouth into a firm line and repeated her newest mantra. There would be a way. Replacing the magazine in its drawer, she reached up and ran her finger across the smooth surface of a barrette. "Mom grew her hair long. I would have liked to have seen that."

Torenz cleared his throat. "Actually, those were Dad's. He said there was no point in cutting his hair because there was no one important stationed here and Mom didn't care."

Denefe's jaw dropped and she stared at him. That was almost verbatim what she'd thought about her uniform at the Brazil Base.

Torenz must have noticed her reaction. "What?"

Sorrow and loss pinged through her. Instead of answering his question, she parried with one of her own. "Which parent are you most like?"

He laughed. "I'm Mom. Through and through."

"Me?"

"That's easy. You're like Dad. Kaleen is like Mom too. Just in a different way than me."

Like Dad. Kaleen was like Mom.

Two halves of the whole.

Denefe began her perusal of the room again. "Why did they leave us behind when they risked taking you as an infant?"

"The plan was for Mom to take me first because I was the strongest of the three of us. Then you two were to come with other members of the team. They made special pouches for us, based on everything they knew about the anomaly at the time. It wasn't enough. I almost died. Mom had to doctor me for a long time. They didn't want to risk it with you two."

"Later? When we were older?"

"By then, our parents were gone. I…didn't think you'd want to be trapped here."

She tried her earlier questions again. "Am I? Trapped here? There's no way home?"

Torenz slowly nodded. "The anomaly is only one way, and the desert is too deep. I'm sorry."

Denefe felt as if she'd been slapped. She stared at the familiar brown eyes and white hair of her brother. "Sorry? My sister is there, in that world! A man who loves me is waiting for me to come back! Do you think you could do better than 'I'm sorry'?"

He let his gaze drop to the floor, breathing hard. He stood like that for a moment. When he did eventually raise his eyes, they were red-rimmed. He spoke softly. "I know what it's like. I was nine years old when I found out I was only one-third of a person, that two-thirds of me was out there, in that world." He pointed to the distant right. "How do you think I felt, knowing I would never be a complete person? That I would always be alone here?" He paused, and when she didn't answer, he continued. "I'm just saying that I know what you're going through. I really do. 'I'm sorry' is the best I've got."

"Why didn't you tell us? *You* could have said something." She tapped her temple.

"I wasn't allowed."

Now it was Denefe's turn to pause in sudden understanding. "GlobeX was listening with their own telepaths." She nodded, thinking back to age seven. That was when she and Kaleen had first noticed people listening in on their telepathic conversations. Suddenly, their fosterage caregivers would know things that they had only told each other. It was when they'd invented their message code.

Torenz said, "Still, I'd listen to your telepathic voices sometimes. It was comforting to me."

Denefe concentrated on the waist-high shelf that ran the perimeter of the room. It was filled with electronic tablets and plain brown books. Pulling one of those latter, she opened it to see neat and concise handwriting. Her parents' journals.

"May I borrow some of these?"

Torenz frowned. "Those are official GlobeX property. I can't loan them until I get official authorization."

She nodded and turned as if to reshelf it. Blocking the view from the door, she slid the journal into her shirt. She shuffled the books on the shelf to hide the gap.

Too bad for GlobeX. Those journals had belonged to *her* parents.

115

Chapter 26
Kaleen's Brother

Pleading tiredness, Denefe returned to her room. She'd been in the underground facility for only a few days, but it felt more like a month. In truth, she was exhausted, even though it wasn't even the middle of the day yet. She needed a nap and privacy to read the journal.

Torenz let her keep the shuttle cart after she promised she wouldn't drive like a maniac. True to her word, she flew it carefully, parking in the corner of her room. She clutched the journal close to her stomach beneath her shirt as she crept to the door and shut it. She'd need a hiding place. Looking around the room, her gaze lit on the bottom drawer of the dresser. It would be one of the first places anyone would look. She needed someplace improbable.

Shuffling to her little shuttle cart, she realized it was the perfect solution. She could send it back to where it belonged and then, when she wanted the journal, she could beg tiredness and have the cart brought to her.

There was no real hiding place in the riding compartment. The gaps beside and beneath the seat were too obvious as was behind the front console. Denefe turned on the machine and then dropped to her knees. With the cart hovering, she saw the bottom was a solid plate. However, there was a small gap toward the front where the tow compartment opened. After flipping it out, she removed the tow cable before she slid the journal in its place. There was just enough room to wedge the cable back in front of it. Perfect.

She turned off the shuttle cart.

She pulled herself to her feet and scooted to the dresser. Face-to-face, as she was, with the down-turned photo of her parents, she hesitated. She understood, now, the reasons for being abandoned. She stood the frame upright on the dresser against the wall. It wasn't their fault. They'd wanted to bring her and Kaleen.

Hanging the photo would wait 'til later. Right now, she was beat.

Once she reached her bed, it took no time for her to fall asleep.

It didn't seem like it lasted long, though. It felt as if almost immediately Kaleen's voice began an incessant chant in her mind. *"Denefe, where are you?"*

"Here. I'm here." Denefe mumbled against her pillow, eyes still closed. Realizing she'd answered only out loud, she struggled to a sitting position. *"I was asleep."*

"Asleep? I thought it would be afternoon there."

"It is. It was just an exhausting morning." She glanced at her nightstand and noted the presence of a food tray. Lunch? Supper? *"At least I* think *it's still afternoon."*

"Do we need to discuss that dress more? Are you done obsessing?"

Did they need to keep to the code? Denefe checked

on Torenz in her mind. He was thinking about someone he spoke with, a paramour? She considered. It was impossible for a telepath to think and read someone at the same time. He seemed plenty distracted with his girlfriend, whoever she was. However, he could periodically stop and check on her, so she'd have to check on him occasionally too. *"No, I'm done with the dress, for now. I think we should keep our conversations to the middle of the night from now on."*

"Okay. I have news. According to the recorder in that metronome, the guy was conducting some kind of investigation into a rumor about an underground city from the future."

Denefe's pulse quickened. Why would someone from Egypt know about an underground city in the Gobi Desert? *"What else?"* She checked on Torenz again. Still deep into flirting.

Kaleen said, *"The recordings are just interviews of people who had heard the legend."*

"No one who has been there?"

"Not that I heard. Do you suppose they're talking about your location?"

"Must be. Which means I'm not in the Gobi Desert. It makes me wonder if this underground city is still there, in your time."

"I can ask around."

She checked Torenz again. Still safe. *"Be careful. It could be a secret base. I've never heard of it. It's called Definitive Headquarters."*

"Gotcha. How are you feeling?"

"Better. I'm mobile at least." She put her hand on her forehead and paused. *"I have news for you too. It seems there's a lot we were told about our family that isn't true."*

"Like what?"

Staring at her parents' photo, Denefe told her sister

118

about them and how they came to be at the facility in the past. *"I'm not sure yet how they died, but I'll find out. Some kind of accident."*

"Wow. Do you know why the people at GlobeX lied to us?"

"Not yet, but I assume it has something to do with what I'm going to tell you next."

"Should I sit down?"

"Maybe. We have a brother." Denefe winced, waiting for Kaleen's reaction, but when her sister said nothing, she told her about Torenz being a triplet, the DNA test, and the reason for the separation of the family. After she finished, they were both silent.

After a few moments, Kaleen said, *"Well, I'm glad I sat for that one. When do I get to meet him?"*

Denefe laughed. *"When? Funny, given our current circumstances."* She checked on Torenz again. He was still happily distracted. *"Kaleen, here's the thing—I'm not sure I entirely trust him."*

"Okay, now the hairs on the back of my neck are standing up straight. Can you tell me why you feel this way?"

"No, not really. He's just cagey. For example, he's been listening to us for years, but has never made any attempt to contact us."

"So...?"

"I don't know. I just think he's hiding a lot from us."

"Like...?"

"Like about our parents. He won't let me borrow their journals. Like about the rift being only one way. That one may be true. He says we're too deep in the desert to try to find a different route home. A desert that he told me was the Gobi, but might not be."

"I see. So, if there is no way to contact anyone outside, how did the legend of the underground city from

the future get started? How did they get you from the outside to the inside?"

"*My point.*" Denefe shrugged as if her sister could see her.

"*Looks like we both have homework.*"

They chatted for a few more minutes and then said goodbye. Denefe lay back down and checked on her brother. His girlfriend must be some kind of girl to keep him so involved for so long. The only one close enough to his age was Jileah.

She didn't remember seeing any possible exits to the desert during Torenz's tour. She'd ask her...brother...for another one and pay more attention. She'd have to tread carefully. Figure out a way to find out what she needed without hitting any of his road blocks.

Of course she wouldn't have to worry about him if Kaleen could find out something about the facility from her end. That would be spectacular.

Chapter 27
Espionage

Torenz wound through the hallways to his secret lab in long, measured strides, his footsteps echoing thickly from the tight, gray walls.

Something was up.

He'd been visiting Jileah, like he occasionally did, and it had gone well. He'd discovered trouble, however, when he headed to his own quarters. Checking in on Denefe, he'd found her in a tizzy about something he couldn't follow, her thoughts all over the place. She'd begin a sentence and stop in the middle of it. Then she'd start a new one.

"Those recordings—"

"What was—"

"Why would—"

"Staphershire—"

He'd turned on a dime and had immediately made for his hidden desk, nodding to people he passed, waving to those deep in their labs, but not stopping to chit-chat. He had a mission. If he was right, his boss would want to know what was going on.

Still, Denefe's mind filled with rapid-fire, fragmented thoughts. Nothing connected. It was as if she was doing it intentionally. Which she would, if she suspected someone was listening. With a growl, he left her mind. He was getting nowhere. There was, however, one word, or rather name, that kept punctuating her thoughts—*Kaleen.*

His sisters had conferred about something.

Denefe may be well practiced in counter-espionage techniques, but Kaleen, who'd had the same training, had no reason to keep up the habit. He shifted his focus to his sister in the future and was immediately rewarded with her out-of-control thoughts.

"I have a brother. A triplet. Our parents didn't die when we were told. Everything's a lie."

The thoughts interrupted into silence, then restarted. It didn't last long.

"Cardenza may not be so bad, but I still can't trust him. Who do I contact to find out about Definitive Headquarters?"

He shook his head. His sisters would have to be stopped. He would handle Denefe, but someone else would have to deter Kaleen.

Turning right, he entered the outer lab, passing the scientist working there, and pressed his remote, bringing the wall down. Stepping across the threshold, he pressed his remote again and the wall reappeared. Today, however, he didn't smile at the magic of the technology.

Chapter 28
Dad's Journals

Denefe's mind couldn't stop whirling around the things she and Kaleen had discussed. When she couldn't reengage her nap again, she fished her father's journal from its hiding place and read. It was written in a strong, masculine slant. She reveled in her father's written voice, having never had it, marking every comma and exclamation point. There had been no journals in her world. There was absolutely nothing. Now she understood why—it had all been transported here.

She paused. Did that make sense? *All* of it was transported there? Assuming her mother would have sold off everything except the bare necessities before they came there, that would still leave a lot of items that had to be hand-transported over. The least of the things would have been clothing for three, including various sizes for a growing baby. Also, she could assume all prior journals had been electronic and condensed to only one or two pads. How did the new journals get there? Who brought them? What about her father's glasses? Any lab equipment and replacement parts. Where were all the people who brought them? If each person was permanently trapped there, as Torenz assured her they all truly were, they would have quite a few personal items of their own to bring. Who brought the extra items?

According to what she knew of rift labs, there should be at least forty people trapped there just due to transportation of items. Where were they all? Furthermore, the facility didn't have the size required to house that many people.

There had to be another way back to her own time. As Denefe read, she munched from the tray by her bed. Cold food was better than no food. She poured through the journal pages, looking for any clue as to what had happened to the people, but she had no luck. It seemed to be concerned mostly with her father's experiments with sidewinders of all types, though there were quite a few entries about arguments with her mom.

She dropped the journal onto her bed in frustration and concentrated on what was left of her meal—a piece of date pie. No ideas came to her while she ate. After she finished, she eased out of bed and then slowly, carefully, placed the journal in its hiding place.

"Torenz."

It took him a moment to answer, and when he did, his telepathic voice was stressed from shock. *"Wow... It's been a long time since someone spoke into my mind."*

"Oh? I somehow thought you'd be the link to the real world."

"Well, besides dealings with Primary."

"So, you'd be linking with someone in a position like mine."

"Yeah, something like that."

"I don't know what time of day it is, but I'm ready to continue our tour when you're able."

"It's mid-afternoon. I'll be right there."

By the time he arrived, she waited in her chariot.

There seemed to be no real organization to the place. Long white hallways jutted out at odd angles from bends and corners of rooms. Torenz told her it was because they'd expanded only when necessary. Each dig was a huge project, so they conserved space as much as possible.

The garden, however, broke all the rules. The moment she stepped through the entrance, she felt as if she was outside. Giant trees stretched and branched to cover the roof. Footpaths wandered among carefully tended beds of vegetables, fruits, and grasses. The air was fresh and clean with a trace of humidity and without any of the canned flavor the rest of the facility had.

As for the labs, there were only four that were fully outfitted. There was also the dining room, several recreational areas, and approximately three dozen private rooms. Still, the tour took until supper time, about three hours. As for her mission, she'd found no trace of the rift, though she'd felt rift spiders scratch her skin in one place. There seemed to be no extra doors that could be concealing an exit tunnel. None of the research areas had been her father's either. Wherever it was, it was well-hidden. She'd need lots of time alone to find it.

Frustrated again, Denefe followed her brother to the dining room where they ate a light meal. No one really stared at her that time. She'd even met quite a few people on her tour. There were a few covert glances, though. Torenz made light chatter, telling her about different people in the facility.

He said, "There are eighteen of us. Eleven are lab techs and researchers. The rest are support."

So, she'd been right in her estimation. "Is Jileah support or researcher with a doctor degree?"

He smiled briefly. "Jileah is our holistic nurse

practitioner."

"Holistic, meaning the 'medicine' she gave me was what?"

"Just herbs she grows in the garden."

"Great." She tried, but she couldn't keep the sarcasm out of her voice.

"Well, do you feel better?"

"Yes, but not due to a bunch of plants."

His smile was hesitant and he looked as if he wanted to speak, but in the end, he concentrated on his food.

Finally, Denefe gathered her nerve and asked, "What happened to our parents? You said it was an accident."

Pointing at her plate, he said, "That's a long story for another time and place. You look a bit pale. Finish eating and I'll get you back to your bed."

She sighed and dug into her roast. She hadn't seen any livestock, so the animals had to be raised locally and brought into the facility. If they came from the future through the rift, more and more people would be trapped there even just as shepherds. "So, where do you get the prime rib? Keep the cows under your pillow?"

"We're a community of researchers. Is it so hard to believe that we could create something that looks and tastes like beef?"

She eyed her meal. Not real meat. Great. Was nothing in the whole facility what it seemed? She pursued no other conversation, but let Torenz idly chatter about whatever suited him. As soon as she finished her plate, they returned to her quarters. Her brother left shortly after, and she bundled into bed, reaching for sleep as soon as her head hit the pillow.

In the dark, late night Ardense's voice woke her up.

"Denefe, wake up! Denefe!"

"What? You sound upset." She rubbed her eyes,

126

struggling to stay awake. Something she wouldn't get used to was the absolute black when the lights were off. At home, there was always some kind of glow, even on the stormiest of nights.

"What did you tell Kaleen to do? Hallen has arrested her."

"Arrested? Hallen?" She sat straight up in bed. Suddenly, she was completely alert.

"Cardenza and some scientist guy from up north are trying to get her released."

"Why was she arrested? What are the charges? She was only going to ask questions."

"Well, her questions got her in trouble."

Denefe was silent. Bade Hallen, someone she'd always assumed was on her side, had arrested her sister. Ergo, he protected that which Kaleen questioned. Or he acted on orders from higher up the predator chain. Either way, she'd overestimated his loyalty to her. Any help he'd given had been to protect the talent, not the people. Bitterness filled her mouth.

"I can't follow your thoughts. What was that about Hallen?"

"Never mind. What does Cardenza say Kaleen did?"

"He doesn't know, but he's furious. He says Hallen won't discuss it with him. He's doing everything he can to get her released. Tell me what's going on so we can get her free."

"Just a minute." She reached into Torenz's mind and found it quiet. Either he was sleeping or meditating. Or, she corrected, he could be listening to her. She gave it a test. *It must be morning.* There was no confirmation or correction from her brother. He wasn't listening. Or he was wise to tricks. Ardense didn't know the code she and Kaleen used, so there was no way to hide the conversation. She was just going to have to risk it.

Quickly, Denefe outlined what little she and Kaleen had discovered. Her muscles ached with adrenaline to do something to save her sister, but there was nothing she could do in her current world of darkness.

"I've never heard of that place either. I'm joining Cardenza tomorrow and I'll tell him everything you said."

"Ardense, be careful. I don't know who we can trust."

"Gotcha. Love you. Bye."

She tried to reach Kaleen, but received no response. That meant her sister was where there was no rift. She called for her boyfriend again.

'Ardense, Kaleen isn't at Primary. I can't reach her."

"I'm not sure if that makes it worse. I'll talk to you as soon as we find out something."

She nodded as if he could see her. *"I'll be waiting."*

The key to getting Kaleen released and herself back to the right time had to be the production of information. There had to be something she could do, trapped in the past. The little shuttle cart sat waiting in its corner. That wasn't an option. It would be impossible to hide with it if she was caught. She'd have to wait to snoop around the facility until she could carry herself on her own two feet. Maybe tomorrow.

For now, she could re-read her father's journal.

Chapter 29
Accused

The sections of the journal that Denefe read offered no clues and soon she fell asleep. Torenz pounded on her door early the next morning. The book lay spread-eagle on the blankets. Hastily, she jammed it beneath her, making her sit crooked. She struggled to find a normal sitting position, putting one leg over the other.

"Denefe! I know you have it! I'm coming in!" He flung open the door. The red flush of his face was made more noticeable by the white of his short hair. "I know you took it. Where have you hidden it?" He glanced at the furniture in the room and then crossed to the big dresser against the wall.

"I took what?"

"The journal. Dad's journal. I *told* you to put it back." He jerked open the top drawer and then tossed her few belongings from side to side. Not finding anything, he thrust his hand behind the drawer and searched the well of darkness there.

Thankful the journal wasn't hidden in the dresser, Denefe said, "Torenz, you saw me put it back. I don't have it." Beneath her, the journal corners bit into her hips.

Her brother shoved the top drawer closed before he yanked the empty second one open. Again, he slid his hand behind, searching the smooth outsides of the drawer and the inside dresser back. With very little weight in it, the piece of furniture rattled harshly at the violence put upon it.

Finding nothing, he slammed that drawer shut and then wrenched the third one open. It became obvious to Denefe that he wasn't planning on stopping the search until he found the book. She decided to try the offensive.

"So, what then? Are you going to search all three pieces of furniture in this room? Then what? Do you want to search me too? I'm sure I've swallowed it and if you cut me open, you'll find it."

He stopped, slowly sliding the drawer shut. Turning, he stared at her.

Not being one to back down, she pressed the point. "Here, search me. Right here, right now." She moved toward the edge of the bed, carefully reaching behind her to make sure the journal was covered.

Torenz held up his hand and shook his head. "No. I'm sorry. I just..." He paused and then, with a deep breath, continued, "I saw you put it back. I *am* sorry." He started toward the door.

"Is that it? Is that all? You come in here, accuse me of stealing from you, disrespect my things, and that's the apology I get?"

He stopped and shrugged. "What else can I do?"

"How about giving me a reason for all this. Tell me why I can't read those journals." She settled back onto the bed, onto the stolen book.

"They belong to GlobeX. They're a security issue."

"No. They belong to you, me, and Kaleen. All three of us. You've had the privilege of reading them already. Now it's my turn."

He pressed his lips into a thin line. Without another word, he left, shutting the door behind him.

Stunned, Denefe sat for a moment, staring at the door. She reached into his mind. Following his thoughts was like reading his own journal. He made no attempt to hide anything. She wondered if he even knew how. Certainly, as the only telepath in the facility, he'd had no need. He hadn't learned intelligence efforts, either. He should have been reading her then, as she read him. Right at that moment, he ranted about her. At least she knew she'd gotten to him.

Slowly, she turned her gaze to the dresser. If that journal had been hiding there... She shuddered. There *had* to be something in the journals or Torenz wouldn't be in such a twist about them.

First, though, she tried to reach Kaleen. That failing, she tried Ardense. Nothing. Sputtering in frustration, she picked up the ancient journal and read again.

She read about her father's experiments, heady stuff she didn't really understand. Though Kaleen probably would have, at least a little. He expressed his hopes and failures. In his slanted script, he wrote about personal things too. He talked about the social events the facility held. He also spoke of personal relationships.

Denefe had a hard time concentrating. She missed Ardense. Her whole life back home. She was deathly worried about her sister.

She needed to hear Kaleen's voice. When the two of them were young, they fought a little until they realized the gulf that grew between them was more painful than any part of the fight. Now, they never fought. This inability to speak with her felt exactly the same.

She hugged her knees to her chest, staring at the pages of the journal, but not really seeing them. What was happening with her twin? Why had she been arrested? What was Hallen hiding? What was Torenz hiding? Why couldn't she reach anyone?

Chapter 30
Bade Hallen

Kaleen sat on an uncomfortable hardwood chair in a room that was no bigger than her tent. The yellowish lighting gave her a headache. She had no idea how long she'd been there, but she'd been sitting for a very long time. Even if she wanted to stretch out to sleep, she couldn't. There was no room. Instead, she'd just drooped into the chair, waiting.

How could she have been so stupid? She'd thought she was being careful, but in retrospect, she'd been more like a charging bull, asking everyone she knew about Definitive Headquarters.

She'd also thought the people she'd spoken to were friends she could trust. So, who'd sold her out?

The door scraped open and a tall, lean fellow in a suit walked in, followed closely by Bade Hallen's short, round bulk. The yellow light sickeningly reflected from their skin, more so from Bade's bald head. The room was cramped with just one person, but now there was no space to move, to avoid the two men in front of her. They seemed to suck out all the air.

She tried to rise to her feet, but quickly sat back

down once she realized she'd be pressed against one of the two men. "Bade! Thank goodness you're here! What's going on? Why have I been arrested?"

Instead of answering, Bade stared at her, as if trying to measure her value. With a sigh, he nodded.

The man beside him shrugged off his coat, no easy feat in such cramped quarters. He handed the suit coat to Bade and began, "What do you know about Definitive Headquarters? Who have you spoken to about it?"

Chapter 31
Dad

Denefe's stomach twisted, rumbling loudly, reminding her she'd most probably missed breakfast as well as her dinner the night before. She had no idea anymore how long she'd been prisoner in the underground facility. She glanced at the walls for a clock she knew wasn't there, then shook her head at the habit and edged out of bed.

Just as she'd finished dressing and had returned the journal to its hiding place, two sharp raps sounded on her door. That wasn't Torenz. His knock didn't sound like that. She hobbled across the room and admitted Jileah, brandishing a cane.

"Oh, good. You're up," the nurse said as she came into the room. "I haven't seen you for a couple of days. How are you feeling?"

"Hungry and lost in time. I need a clock. Or at least food that looks like a clock."

Jileah laughed. It was a loud, hearty laugh, not a simpering whimper like lots of women had. She handed Denefe the cane. "I can take care of both those things. First, food. Come with me."

Shambling to keep up with Jileah's patient walk, Denefe said, "Torenz tells me you're a holistic healer."

"I just don't see the point in subjecting injuries like yours to more trauma via chemicals or invasive surgery, especially when there's no emergency."

Made sense. Sorta. "I might have healed quicker."

"Are you going somewhere?" The nurse laughed again, a sound Denefe found she liked very much. It made her wish they could become friends.

"Well, I'd like to go home. Go shopping, to the movies, or even to the gym. You know." They turned a corner.

"You can't do that. I thought Torenz told you. The anomaly is only one way, and we have no means of transport that will take us out of the desert." A frown creased Jileah's face.

"He told me, yes, but I have a hard time believing him when I see all the equipment here. Someone had to bring it all. So, where are they? What about you? I assume you were born here or brought as a baby. Where'd you and Torenz get your training?"

Jileah stopped in the middle of the long, white hallway, a shocked look on her olive-skinned face. "He hasn't told you about the accident?"

Denefe glanced both ways, but there was nobody waiting to get past or otherwise. So, she just stood there too. "Accident? No. I mean, he told me that my parents both died in one, but not what occurred."

Shaking her head, the nurse's thick brown hair fell into her eyes. She smoothed the lock away, and said, "It's not for me to tell. He should be the one." She started to walk on, but Denefe caught her arm.

"Please. Torenz and I...are having trouble adjusting to each other. This is something I need to know. Please tell me."

Jileah nodded. "You and your brother are a lot

136

alike, I think. I'm not surprised you're having trouble." She turned to continue down the hallway, and Denefe hobbled beside her. "Your father was a brilliant man. Amazingly so. He was articulate. When he'd explain something technical, you'd have no problem following him. He made you feel smart too." Sorrow filled her face. "I was only nine when I was sent here with my mother. Despite my age, your father befriended me. I miss him. He was a friend. He's the one who taught me about herbal remedies. They were a hobby of his."

For a moment, Denefe thought that was all she was going to get. The scent of food trickled through the hall and strengthened when they turned left around a corner. Jileah squared her shoulders and continued her story as they took another immediate right.

"He was working on doubling the anomaly. Making it go both ways. Everyone was devoted to the project, including your mother when she wasn't training Torenz. All resources were dedicated to him. Nothing was spared. Still, it took almost three years before they were ready to implement any theories.

"The first tests went well. Your father was able to reverse a tiny spot in the anomaly enough to send a mouse through. The trouble was, the process didn't last long and the mouse didn't make it to the other side. The poor creature was spit back out within seconds, burned to a crisp. It was a beginning.

"The next step involved making the reversal last longer. It took over a year to get from theory to application. When they finally proceeded with the tests, things went well. This time they were able to get a mouse all the way to the other side, alive. Everything looked so promising. Everybody was laughing and giddy. That night we all had a party to celebrate.

"In the morning, your father's team began working on the problem of expanding the size of the reversal.

The process took approximately five years with many failed tests. Early on, there was one breakthrough when they were able to make the reversal one-tenth bigger. Again, we all celebrated, but that was the end of the success. Nothing tried after that would work. Many, including your mother, thought it would be impossible to enlarge the reversal too much more, but your father was adamant it would work. In the end, he found your mother was right. Once in place, an anomaly or reversal was stuck at the same relative size. One made the size of a mouse could only be made big enough for a larger mouse. At that time, your father still didn't know that. So he kept working.

"Another year, his team had a theoretical reversal the size of a man ready to be tested. This test was to use a lot more energy than any of the previous tests, but your father was confident the anomaly could stand it. As they ramped up the power, the anomaly splintered. Sidewinders shot everywhere, many within the lab. Over thirty people, including your parents and my mother, were killed or went missing. We sealed off the damaged area and the anomaly has been untouchable and shooting sidewinders since."

Denefe said, "I'm so sorry about your mother." Her head swam. Over thirty people dead or missing. The sidewinders that ravaged the planet were being spawned from this one wormhole. Her parents' fault.

Jileah shrugged. "Thank you, but it was a long time ago."

"The rift is untouchable, how?"

"Each time someone tries to run a test, it splinters more. We don't dare try anything now."

They'd reached the dining room, and the conversation paused as they served themselves. The offering for the noon meal was ham, or ham substitute, cooked with stewed figs and onions, some kind of leafy green, and bread full of grains and toasted seeds. Denefe took a sampling of everything.

It was early for the lunch meal and the dining area was still empty. They had their choice of tables and decided on one near the door. Once settled, Denefe asked, "Why is this place called Definitive Headquarters?"

"This is where it all began. It's the first anomaly. The others are just stabilized sidewinders that splintered from this one. Primary was built around the other end of this one."

The answer didn't satisfy Denefe and left her feeling like a wet rag had suddenly descended over the whole thing. She knew this already from Torenz. Yet, she couldn't shake the feeling there was more to the place, something hidden below the surface. Perhaps something Jileah didn't even know. This would be something to pursue again later. She took a hesitant bite of the fake ham, surprised to find it quite realistic. She swallowed, and said, "Come to think of it, I haven't seen the rift anywhere. I assumed it was just Torenz being cagey."

"It's in the damaged section of the lab."

"The one that's sealed off?"

Jileah nodded while finishing a piece of toast.

Another thought hit Denefe. "That was my father's lab that was sealed off, right? Is there any way I can see it?"

A doubtful look spread across the nurse's face as she buttered another piece of toast. "I can check, but don't hold your breath."

"Thanks. It would mean a lot. Torenz has been so cagey. He won't let me anywhere near my parents' stuff. I just want to get to know them a little better." Denefe hated lying to her new friend, but she had to find a way home and her father's lab just might hold the key.

139

Chapter 32
News

That night, Denefe stretched her muscles on the rumpled bed as she prepared to go exploring. She bent her right leg back and curled it over the extended left leg. The walk to and from the dining hall had exhausted her. By the time she'd returned to her quarters, her legs were heavy and unwilling to even stand and a deep tremor had shaken her abdomen. She'd opted for her evening meal in her room. Still, it had felt good to use her body again.

She switched legs. Her long, white hair kept falling in her face. Finally, out of frustration, she coiled it on top of her head and pushed a pencil through it.

Jileah had brought the evening meal, but instead of leaving afterward, had stayed and chatted. She'd turned out to be a good companion, and Denefe found she liked the nurse's company a great deal.

The conversation about the accident had answered a few questions. It explained why the sidewinder had nearly reversed itself in location when she was taken. As this was the original wormhole, all sidewinders, including ones like that which had snatched her, had a connection, somehow, to this region.

Denefe tucked both feet under her hips and arched backward, putting her upper body weight onto her hands behind her, and stretching her aching abdomen.

Jileah's story also confirmed what Torenz had told her—there was no way home through that wormhole. Denefe paused. Unless they lied. That was what she was going to find out shortly.

She relaxed a moment and then stretched backward again.

Shifting her mind, she called for Kaleen. Still not receiving an answer, she called Ardense. There was no response there either. Where were they? She sputtered her lips, pushing away the worry. It would be all right in the end. It had to work out, somehow.

She stretched her abdomen a third time and then reached for Torenz's mind, listening, but found him completely silent. If he was asleep, there would be fragments of dream thoughts. Either he meditated or he listened also. To his contact or to her?

Quadruplet, she tried in her mind only. There was no correction within him. Ergo, he wasn't listening to her. Who was his contact? Was he listening at all? She waited, watching his silence. She couldn't begin her mission if her brother was awake. Patience was Kaleen's strong suit, not hers. She much preferred beating something senseless until it worked right. That included people. Frustrated, she leaned back onto her pillow to wait.

Finally, she felt his mind busy itself with the preparations of bed. As it quieted into sleep and disjointed dream thoughts, she stood and moved toward the door. As slowly as she walked, he ought to be deep into his dreams by the time she got halfway down the hall.

Unlike her Brazil Station, there appeared to be no

night shift here. The offices and labs she passed were dark and silent. She liked being the only person out and about. There was something oddly comforting about it.

She rounded the last corner and gazed upon her destination. Even now she felt the sharp tingles of the rift spiders.

Ardense's voice sounded in her mind. *"Denefe."*

She crept toward the shadows of the lab, banging her hip on the sharp corner of the center counter as she moved behind it. A lance of pain shot down her leg to her foot, numbing it. Sucking in her breath, she leaned against the wall behind her and slid to the floor. Light from the hallway spilled into the lab and shadows from scientific equipment made strange dark creatures beside her. She stared at them, rubbed her hip, and asked, *"Where are you? What happened? Where's Kaleen? Is she okay?"*

"Whoa! One at a time. Kaleen's fine. They let me see her. She's furious. Cardenza has really gone to bat for her. It looks like she might be released soon."

Denefe frowned. *"Where are you now?"*

"Cardenza sent me back home again. There's nothing I could do. He thought it better that I stay near a rift opening to keep in contact with you." His telepathic voice was soft and it faded in and out from weariness. She concentrated to follow his answer.

"So what happened? Why do they have Kaleen prisoner?"

"I don't know. They wouldn't tell any of us the charges. I got the definite impression she didn't want to discuss anything because of eavesdroppers."

Chapter 33
Busted

Frustration filled Denefe and she sputtered her lips. If only she could be there! Maybe she wouldn't have been able to help. If Kaleen was worried someone listened in on her conversation with Ardense, she was probably worried about telepathic ones too. *"What about Cardenza? Can we trust him?"*

"Do we have a choice? He agrees something's not right."

Ardense had a point, but still... *"They have my twin! How not right does it have to be?"*

"I don't know, Denefe. Don't kill the messenger." His telepathic voice turned churlish.

She took a deep breath. He was right. Of course. *"I'm sorry. Is there any way you can find out how much Cardenza knows?"*

"I can try."

"Ardense...be careful."

"I love you too."

Denefe stood and walked silently along the gray lab wall, stepping over cords and lines and dodging tables in the dim room. She slid around the corner of the last worktable and reached the back wall. Painful stings like angry ant bites rippled across her, announcing the nearby presence of the damaged rift.

Sliding her hands across every smooth inch of the wall, she searched for a hidden keyhole, indentation, or notch of some kind. Failing to find anything, she searched the corners and adjoining walls. Still nothing.

Denefe stepped back and critically surveyed the wall. The door to the rift couldn't open from somewhere else. According to the rift spiders biting her skin, this was the closest room of any kind. There had to be something.

"It uses a laser code."

Denefe whirled to find Torenz standing in the hall, just outside the lab. He didn't look surprised to see her.

She stared at him. His lean, athletic body and white hair were so like her own. She stayed where she was, her hands on her hips, waiting as he walked in. "You spying on me?"

"I couldn't settle into a good sleep, so I went to see if you were still awake too. Imagine my surprise to find you gone."

She jerked her thumb toward the wall, and said, "I want in there."

He shook his head, his short haircut waving back and forth at the vehemence. "Nope. In light of your excursion tonight, your request to see Dad's lab is denied."

"Then I want to talk to the person in charge." She lifted her chin.

"No one's in charge." He frowned and pulled a tall stool from the other side of the counter into the middle of the lab. A second stool joined the first. He patted it.

He didn't honestly think she'd sit next to him, did he? That was a bit too arrogant, even for him. "No one?"

"They're all dead."

145

All dead. Well, that was just genius. That was a long time ago. Someone must have taken their places. Denefe tried a different approach. "Who has the laser tag?"

Torenz pressed his lips thin, but didn't answer.

"So, you have the ability to enter, but you're not going to let me in to my own parents' lab?"

"We both know your drive to enter that lab has nothing to do with any desire to learn anything about them. You want access for only one reason—to test the anomaly and see if I'm lying."

Now it was Denefe's turn to remain quiet. She felt her face flame and looked away.

"I can't let you tamper with it. It's damaged enough."

"Torenz, who's your contact on the other side? Who's your employer?"

He shook his head, his lips tight again.

When it became obvious he wasn't going to answer her question, she decided to give up for the time being and they lulled into silence. After a long time, Torenz stirred, stood, and stretched. "I'm going to bed. I'd like my book back, first, though."

Denefe frowned. "What book?"

An ugly sneer twisted across his face, then vanished. "Don't play games. It's restricted property. Give it back."

She smiled sweetly. "When I'm finished reading *our* father's book."

Chapter 34
Spies

Torenz shook his head as he walked away. Denefe was just like Dad. Stubborn to a fault. What if he and his sisters had grown up under one roof? Would they be close? Or would their personal liabilities, like Denefe's stubbornness, have driven them apart?

He let himself dwell on that thought until he realized he couldn't hear Denefe's footsteps echoing like his in the long halls. He stopped and listened but heard nothing. She was still at the lab.

He pressed his lips tight and turned on his heel, his shadow leading the way back, but when he reached the lab, Denefe was nowhere to be seen. He reached for her mind and found it as a tightly compacted ball with no way for him to enter. Someday, he was going to have to get her to teach him how to do that.

He heard her footsteps receding in the hallway he'd just left. She had to have waited in a different lab for him to pass. Had she been in his mind? Spying on him while he spied on her?

Fury erupted within him. After all her indignation, her self-righteousness, and scolding about him reading her mind without permission!

Well, there was more than one way to skin a cat. He couldn't connect with Kaleen due to her location, so he reached through time, stretching his thoughts for Denefe's boyfriend. The moment he touched Ardense's mind, it snapped up into a tight ball.

Obviously, his sister had warned her boyfriend.

Torenz hissed through bared teeth.

Chapter 35
It's What?

Long after Denefe returned to her room, she lay awake. She'd checked on Torenz several times since their meeting. It took a while for him to fall asleep, his mind filled with the disjointed thoughts of what it felt like to have family again and all the frustrations associated with it.

She had to find a way into the restricted area. She didn't believe Torenz, or Jileah, for that matter, about the rift's fragile state or one-way-ness. Not only did she need to see the rift and test it herself, but she suspected there were other secrets that area contained. For one, she'd still seen no evidence of an external exit anywhere else. There had to be one, even if only into the desert. It had to be in there. So, first, she had to get the laser tag from Torenz.

Or, she corrected, she had to find a way to bypass it.

"Ardense." She had to call him three times before he answered.

"Denefe, do we have to talk right now? I'm exhausted. I'm trying to catch up on my sleep." The weariness wound through his telepathic voice. She felt

bad for him, but she needed him.

"It's the middle of the night here. Yes, I need to speak at this time. It's too dangerous during the day. I need you to find out something." There was no answer. Had he fallen asleep? *"Ardense?"*

"Hmm? What?"

"I need you to ask Mik something."

"If it's not life and death, tell me about it tomorrow night." He abruptly left the conversation.

"Ardense! Do you want me to wake you every hour, or do you want to end this conversation quickly?"

He sighed. *"If you were here right now, I'd throttle you!"*

"Feeling's mutual, dear."

"Okay. I'll write it on my comm so I don't forget it. You know, in case my memory suffers from sleep deprivation. God forbid."

She grinned at the sarcasm. *"Ask Mik how to bypass a laser tag lock."*

"That's it? You woke me for that?"

"Yes, I did. I need it as soon as possible. Thank you."

"Throttle you. Do you understand?"

"Sweet dreams." There was no response. He was gone, and she wasn't sure he'd even heard her final message.

Denefe tried to sleep, but she was still too keyed up. Why was no one at GlobeX upset that she was suddenly in the past? The answer came to her immediately—because all the important stuff happened here. What was it?

Were she and Kaleen just spare parts? Being saved in case they were needed in a different location. Was that why they held her sister in an isolated prison—to safeguard her?

Her mind went around and around, asking herself

those questions over and over, trying to find answers. Sleep never came.

According to the clock Jileah had given her, it was almost seven in the morning when Kaleen contacted her.

"Denefe, I'm here."

Denefe's eyes snapped open from her latest attempt at sleep. *"Kaleen! Are you okay?"* A flood of worry flowed out of Denefe, and she was surprised her eyes filled with tears. She hurriedly checked on Torenz. Still sleeping.

"Yes. I'm fine." Kaleen sounded terse.

"What happened? Why did they arrest you?"

"Treason. Can you believe it?"

"What?" Denefe wasn't sure she'd heard right. Treason usually involved spies. *"Hallen can't arrest you for that. He can only make citizen arrests."*

"Apparently, Bade Hallen is military."

"Military? GlobeX must be just a cover corporation. It's the only thing that makes sense." She thought back to Torenz in his room, listening to someone or something. *"Torenz isn't just reporting data from the researchers, he must be a spy. The past is the perfect hiding place. He'd never be found."*

"I'll bet there are unknown telepaths that have carefully been worked into key positions throughout the world."

The thought sobered Denefe. She stared at the wall beside her bed. Her brother was a military spy. *"How did Cardenza get you out?"*

"He threatened Hallen. He said too many people knew about me. He'd go public with all the information and let the media sort it out."

"Do you think Cardenza's someone we can trust?"

"I hate to admit it, but yes."

Imagine that. Trusting Cardenza. She'd been told twice now that they could. Denefe shook her head. What

151

was the world coming to? *"Spies."*

"Yep. We know what that means."

It meant they'd have to stay strictly in code. *"Yeah, we do. It also means you're going to have to visit Brazil Base."* To warn Ardense, was her unfinished message. Kaleen would figure that out.

"I'll hop on the next plane."

"Kaleen, Cardenza is key. Also, remember Starry in your prayers."

Chapter 36
Truth and Lies

Denefe frowned. Everything would depend on Kaleen. She had to coordinate everyone, figure out what needed to be discovered, and handle all the coded conversations. It was a lot, but she was sure Kaleen was up to the task.

Meanwhile, all Denefe could do was sit there, trapped in the past. For the past seven days and the foreseeable future. At that thought, her heart beat like a stampeding horse and suddenly her room seemed way too small. She launched out of bed and reached for the door before she realized how well she moved. Experimentally, she touched her toes. There was very little pain. She straightened and twisted sideways in both directions and then pulled each knee up to her chest, one-by-one. Very little pain, indeed. It seemed she was healed.

With a satisfied smile, she pulled open her door and almost plowed into Jileah, who stepped back a couple of feet, blinking rapidly, her thick brown brows arching in surprise.

"I was just coming to see how you felt this

morning," Jileah said, pulling small pieces of lint off Denefe's shirt.

Denefe's heart slowed to a normal pace. "I feel great. I'm not very sore at all. Want to go shopping at the mall with me?"

A slow smile spread across the other woman's olive-colored face and she chuckled. "Sure. We can have an early breakfast at this great new restaurant, 'The Gobi Dunes.'"

"Sounds yummy. Let's go." Denefe forced her own smile. Was it possible that Jileah really didn't know anything about the truth? She hooked her arm through her friend's, and they marched down the hall, giggling at their game.

At the dining room, they gave exotic names to their dishes and sat at a corner table, pointing out a make-believe window and laughing at the other diners who they pretended were also shoppers.

In a lull, Denefe asked, "So, what does a holistic nurse do in her spare time?"

"You mean, besides shop?" The nurse laughed. She waved one of her large hands. "Well, there are station duties we all take turns doing, like cooking or cleaning common areas. That sort of thing. Also, there are always a few game tournaments to play or watch. Oh, and we have a few vids on private comms."

"Speaking of which, is there one I can use?" Seeing Jileah's skeptical look, Denefe continued, "I used to keep my life in mine. You know, a journal and things like that."

Slowly the tall woman across from her nodded. "I suppose I can wrangle one up for you."

"Thank you. I've been going nuts without one." Changing subjects, she asked, "So, where do people work out? I haven't seen an exercise room or gym anywhere."

154

"That's because you've only visited my office once—the day you almost wrecked that shuttle cart." Jileah added, "Not that I blame you. You had every right to be that traumatized."

"Yeah, I guess so." Denefe looked up at her new friend. "I'm sorry I tricked you into answers that first day. I haven't tried to read your thoughts since and I won't do it again without your permission."

Jileah smiled and reached across the table for Denefe's hand. "It's okay. You were scared, and I'm sure I would have done the same thing."

Denefe marveled at the woman's easy forgiveness. She wasn't so sure she'd have been as understanding. "I'm glad we're friends, and I'm glad you're dating my brother."

"I'm glad we're friends too, but your brother and I aren't dating. At least not on my end."

"Ah. One of those where he thinks the relationship is more than it is."

"Oh, I see you're familiar with it. Not that I really blame him, there's a shortage of women his age down here." She scrunched her nose, then sighed and said, "You want to go see that gym now?"

Together, they walked to Jileah's office where, true to her word, Denefe found an attached room filled with weights of all kinds. They worked out for over an hour. What hadn't been sore on Denefe's body before was now. They parted with plans for supper.

After she reached her quarters, she settled onto the bed and waited nearly four hours until Torenz—who was well awake and showed no signs of sleep—was preoccupied. There had to be a better way to do this! She called Ardense. *"Are you there?"*

"Hey, you." He sounded strong and refreshed.

"I see you're in a better mood."

"Amazing what a few hours of sleep can do for a

temperament."

Denefe ignored the sarcasm. *"Kaleen's on her way to you."*

"She arrived about an hour ago." After a short hesitation, he asked, *"How are you? I miss you, you know."*

"Yeah, I know. I can't wait to see you again. I'm good, I guess. Er, no. Scratch that. I'm going crazy with inactivity. I've found the gym, so that takes the edge off, but still…"

"You can't wait to get back."

"You said it." Denefe decided to bite the bullet. She wondered, briefly, if she needed a code, but decided against it. This conversation could be handled in other ways. *"Has Kaleen brought you up to speed?"*

He answered slowly, carefully. *"She's told us about her time in jail and her reunion with you."*

His words were innocuous, but carried a weight of worry and meaning.

"Did Kaleen bring Bridger with her?"

"She did, but Denefe…" His voice was skeptical.

"You can trust him." That Kaleen brought Bridger was good news. It meant she'd understood that the message about Starry had been really been about the microchip.

Ardense was silent.

She said, *"When I get back home, I may not be working for GlobeX. You could quit with me."* Would he understand that she spoke about hiding from the company?

"What will I do without GlobeX? We don't have enough money for our own company yet."

"You'll be with me. We'll be together. We'll find more work."

"It's a big decision. I'm not ready for this."

Big decision? He had to decide if he cared for her

156

more than GlobeX? *"Okay. I'll talk to you later."* She left the conversation before he could tell her he loved her.

Chapter 37
Everything is Wrong

Denefe watched Torenz watching someone. It was still the evening of her seventh day trapped below ground, the same day she'd told Ardense he had to make a choice. Even hours later, she was still in a foul mood from the conversation. It only added to her angst that she'd been a captive in the facility for so long she'd lost track of the days of the week. Had it been a Monday or Tuesday that she'd been snatched by the sidewinder? There was no sunlight, nor fresh breeze. No way to tell. She was trapped underground with all the weight of the world bearing down on her from above.

Inside her mind, she felt her brother waiting and listening. To whom? She scowled and decided to bite the bullet. *"Care to explain why you're spying on me?"*

The answer was prompt. *"I don't trust you."*

"Ha! That's a laugh coming from you. You act like you're king here in the Gobi Desert."

Torenz's mind immediately made the automatic correction—*"Egyptian."*

Denefe was quiet a moment, letting her sibling soak in that she'd uncovered another lie. *"Why are you telling everyone it's the Gobi?"*

Instead of answering, he parried with a question of his own. *"How'd you find out?"*

She didn't answer.

He gave a mental sigh. *"We told them that because there are no known anomalies near there. We had to keep people from trafficking in and out."*

"So you told them all a lie."

"Coming here is a one-way ticket."

"I'm not supposed to be here."

"Doesn't matter. I can't let you expose us." Regret was clear in his voice.

"You may be a triplet, but you're not our brother." With that, Denefe left the conversation and blocked him from her mind. It was childish, she knew, but she just couldn't help herself. She actually hated him. How could someone so genetically close to her be such a liar?

She felt miserable all over. There she was, trapped in the past with a brother who wasn't. She couldn't find her way home, except through a locked passage that she may or may not be able to access. Her sister might as well be on another planet for all the closeness they could share with someone spying on them, not to mention the danger stalking them all. Her boyfriend wanted to be with her forever, but only if it was on his terms. Her parents were totally different than what she'd been told.

That about summed up everything. Sputtering her lips, she paced her floor and then bolted out her door for the peace of exercise.

By the time she returned to her room, a comm lay on her bed with the note, *It's an old one, but it still works. Put it to good use. J.*

Denefe smiled. She intended to put it to very good use. She turned it on and ran through its programs and operating system. It wasn't just old. It was a dinosaur. As much as she hated speaking to Ardense again at the

159

moment, she should alert Mik not to make the program too difficult.

"Ardense."

"What do you need, Denefe?"

"Please tell Mik that the comm I have is a relic." She actually hoped Torenz listened at that moment. Let him wonder what she was doing.

"Got it," he began. *"Denefe, I—"*

"Gotta go. Bye!" She hoped he would just leave. Even though she could block him from her mind, some small part of her didn't want to draw that final line. Didn't want to force the relationship to be over.

After a moment, his voice came again. *"Okay, then. Love you. Bye."*

When he'd gone, longing filled her just to hear his voice again. She wanted to be home and feel his breath on her hair while he held her the way only he did. Why did her relationships always come to an end?

Tears suddenly overwhelmed her. She twisted on the bed and burrowed her face into her pillow, letting the sobs come. She hated this place!

The emotional drainage and her sleepless night took their toll on her and soon she found herself fighting to keep her eyes open. After the fifth time of jerking herself awake, she finally gave in and tucked herself under the blankets, cradling the comm in both hands, close to her chest. Her last thought was of Kaleen and the expression on Hallen's face when the two of them would eventually expose him and this whole mess to the world.

Chapter 38
Shut Out

Torenz snarled in frustration. He jumped to his feet, sending dust bunnies scuttling across the floor. He stared into the depths of the violet wormhole, ignoring the painful tingles all across his skin and the harsh ozone smell. *"What do you mean it isn't my concern?"*

The telepath from the future said, *"Exactly what I said. The troubles your sisters are causing and our plans of action are none of your business. Your job is to ride herd on Denefe. When you need to sleep, another telepath will take over with her. That's the extent of your worries. Do you understand?"*

"Perfectly!" Torenz gritted his teeth and stormed away from the whirling anomaly, out of his office, and through his father's old lab, pressing the laser remote for the wall. Why wouldn't his boss, Bade Hallen, want his help? He was the strongest telepath they had, bar none, even stronger than Denefe.

It wasn't until he crossed the threshold of the wall and it reappeared, hiding the lab, that he realized the answer—because Denefe was his sister.

The other telepaths spied on him too.

Chapter 39
Puppy

Kaleen stared at the message on the comm. Black letters on a pale background. She'd portioned Mik's instructions to different members of Denefe's team, asking them to insert innocuous words in place of the mathematical elements.

She'd used the physical layout of Brazil Base as the frame reference for the equations, thereby lessening the danger of telepaths learning their mission. The result was a story such as she might tell her sister while just chatting. The message was too long for their normal code. All she had to do was read directly from the comm screen. True, it was daytime, but the spies could be listening any time.

She looked at Ardense, who stood at a large window overlooking the rainforest outside their building. After a moment, he turned and, catching her eye, nodded.

Stepping closer to the silver rift and hoping any listening spies wouldn't understand the conversation, Kaleen reviewed the words written on the comm again. It wasn't a code or ruse they'd ever used, but she felt confident Denefe would understand the hidden message. There was only one thing in the world her twin was allergic to.

"Denefe, are you there? Guess what, I got a puppy on my way to Brazil Base. The moment I put it down, it ran all the way to the cafeteria…"

Chapter 40
The Rift

In the early pre-dawn hours of Denefe's ninth day at Definitive Headquarters, and a full day after she received the code from Kaleen, she stood in front of the plain lab wall, holding her comm. The way home could lay behind there.

She was giddy from exhaustion and the emotional overload, still, from Ardense. Twice, while she'd been entering the initial code, she'd had to erase what she'd typed and begin again, without thinking on what she was doing. Not to mention the many breaks and confusions she'd thrown in for telepathic listeners. Finally, the program had come to life on the small screen. Now she was about to test it on the wall.

She typed in the activation code, pointed the comm, and pushed her thumb onto the execute button.

Nothing happened.

She snapped closed the comm and then flicked it back on again. The seconds clicked by painfully slow. Torenz was still asleep, but he was restless and could wake up. The comm whirred to life, and she once again typed in the activation code.

Stepping closer, she pressed the execute button and held the comm's face toward the wall. Still nothing. Slowly, she walked forward, still holding the comm aloft. Four feet away, the wall suddenly dissipated.

"Alakazam," Denefe whispered and stepped through. Dim lights came up immediately. Rift spiders increased ten-fold, swarming across her skin. Turning behind her, she waved her magic comm and the wall reappeared. She smiled.

"Take that, Torenz!"

Turning around again, she surveyed the room. This had been her father's lab. It looked like the one she'd just left. Same tables, same cabinets, same sink, but it differed with the sheer ton of dust and lack of any equipment. The place was devoid of any personality that suggested her father too. It almost disappointed her, but then, there *was* a door on the back wall. The closer she came to it, the quicker the rift spiders crawled across her skin.

The door opened into a short bay, complete with a skimmer parked near a large utility door at the far end. There was a passageway to the right, leading to what the rift spiders told her was the correct direction. She followed that until she came to another door.

Opening it, Denefe found herself facing a small metal desk and chair. Next to it was a tall, empty bookcase. Footsteps tracked in the dust back and forth and across the room. On the left wall was the wormhole. She wasn't sure what she'd been expecting, but it was massive, much bigger than any she'd ever seen, and brilliant violet, like the sparks had been in the Brazil Base facility. That wasn't good.

Jileah had said it had splintered, shooting off sidewinders everywhere. This was the reason for all the rogue wormholes that ripped across the planet, destroying property and killing people like Starry.

Something had to be done about it, but first, she had to test if it really was one-way.

Seeing nothing to throw, she backtracked to the lab, but found nothing there either. She searched the bay. The giant door at the end tempted her. Was it the way out? The skimmer suggested so. It would be an exploration for another night, if need be. Denefe continued her search. Inside the small craft, she found a small piece of clotted sand. It would have to do.

She returned to the giant anomaly, took a deep breath, and chucked the clod.

It ricocheted violently off the surface of the rift amidst violet sparks, whizzing so close past Denefe's head she was powdered with dust when it embedded in the wall behind her. It was very one-way. No exit.

The rift spiders intensified, becoming painful bites. What was coming next couldn't be good.

Denefe lunged out the door, glancing behind her, just as a writhing violet vortex shot out and swept the room, scoring across the floor. It disappeared.

She leaned against the doorjamb, staring into the room, her limbs shaking as if they remembered the prior journey on their own. If she'd been caught in that, who knew where she would have landed, if she survived.

The original rift had turned a darker, royal purple with streaks of blue in it. She'd damaged it further with one test. What damage had she done to the planet?

Dejected, she returned to the bay and what lay beyond it.

Other than being dusty, the skimmer seemed to be in good working order. She powered it up and gave it a quick run around the bay. The fuel cells were full and the steering moved with easy motion. Someone took care of it.

She could do it. Just run away. Carefully, Denefe turned it off and regarded it. The skimmers didn't have a lot of distance to them. Kaleen's had reached its limit during the trip to her Siberian camp.

Denefe had no idea the distance to the nearest settlement, nor did she know which direction. She could end up stranded with the skimmer. There would be no way to rescue her this time. She'd die from exposure. No. Once was painful enough. She needed a plan and a few supplies

Denefe stepped away from the skimmer before temptation overran her and she bolted with it, heedless of the consequences. Besides, it was nearly morning. There wasn't much time before people would wake up and find her.

She turned to leave, but spotted a DNA lock hidden in the recesses of the handle holding the giant door shut. She needed to return to her room right away, but still she stooped and rubbed her hands in the dust. She'd beaten those kinds of locks before. She just had to confuse it enough. It helped that her DNA was similar to Torenz's. It should be a snap.

Grinning, she pressed her filthy thumb against the pad on the lock. The lock flashed a blue light—not approved. Wiggling her thumb a few seconds brought the desired result. The lock turned green and the door opened, exposing a long, curving hallway with muted light at the end. Chill night air gusted into the bay, carrying with it the smells of sand and desert creatures. This was definitely the way out. To be explored another time. For now, she had to get back to her quarters before people started roaming the halls.

Chapter 41
Trapped

Denefe listened with her ear pressed against the coded wall. Just when she decided the room outside was clear and she could take down the partition, she heard a man softly mutter.

Her luck had run out. Someone was in the lab on the other side.

What now? She couldn't stay locked up all day. Jileah most likely would come looking for her. Not to mention Torenz. Sooner or later, she would be missed.

She leaned against the flat gray of the wall, keeping her ear firmly pressed to it. Time ticked by slowly. Twice she was convinced the scientist had left his lab, only to be startled by some noise of his the moment before she pressed the execute button. After the second time, she slumped to the floor, her head against the wall. It was getting to be a long wait. The man had the constitution of a camel. It seemed he didn't need a break to eat or use the facilities.

Then she heard Torenz.

He and the scientist engaged in an animated conversation, almost as if they argued. Torenz sounded as if he gave orders, and the scientist didn't like them. The voices traveled back and forth throughout the lab, and Denefe pictured the scientist moving around, still working, trying to avoid her brother while Torenz followed him around the lab.

At one point, their voices sounded right on the other side of the wall and she jerked back. Torenz said, "I don't care what it costs you professionally. You're never leaving here, so getting papers published is moot for you. You won't be able to lecture on them, anyway. If you continue to stonewall us, any advancements you hope to make will disappear under your name and reappear under someone else's. Do you understand?"

"You can't do that." The scientist sounded sullen.

"We can and will, buddy. So get off your high horse and get moving on our project." The voices moved off and drifted to a mumble. The scientist sounded contrite and subdued. Torenz became soothing and giving and then disappeared altogether.

Silence once again fell on the lab, with the exception of the occasional mumble.

At last, she heard the scientist yawn long and loud. His muffled footsteps left the lab. Like a shot, Denefe was on her feet, pressing the execute button. The wall evaporated, she stepped through, and rematerialized the wall behind her. At the door, she paused and checked for sounds before bolting into the hallway. If she went directly back to her quarters, she was sure to be caught. Torenz was somewhere close, but there was nothing else that way but the labs.

Where to go?

At the first junction, she turned to the right, keeping to the outskirts of the compound. Eventually, she'd come to someplace that was conceivable she'd visited. What she was looking for came in two more junctions— the gardens. Denefe turned into them.

Leaves scattered the paths. She picked up a few, crushed them, and sprinkled them onto a bench. She sat on them, wiggling a bit to get the flecks imbedded into the seat of her pants. On her comm, she wrote a few lines of drivel about home and lonely love.

All that done, Denefe stood again and walked slowly toward her quarters. How could she be related, a triplet no less, to such a cold man as Torenz? What were he and Hallen doing? Who else was involved? She was so preoccupied in her thoughts she didn't see Torenz until he appeared right in front of her.

"What I'm up to is none of your business. Neither are my associates." He smirked at her start. "Where have you been?"

"Writing in the garden." She lifted her comm by way of explanation.

"Writing, huh? What kind of thing?" He took her comm and read what she'd tossed onto it. "Not bad. I can't write to save my soul."

"It's poor writing. I don't much care for it, but it's kinda how I feel right now." She tried her best disarming smile.

He turned to walk with her. "So, where did you get the idea I was up to something?"

"Aren't you?"

He pursed his lips and then asked again.

Instead of answering, she said, "Torenz, I'm trying really hard to ignore the fact that you read my thoughts uninvited *again*, even after your promises to the contrary. I'm also trying to forget that you lie to me whenever you see fit. You avoid me most of the time. When we *do* get together, we seem to do nothing but argue. You're my brother, and I'm trying to remember that. Do you think you can too?"

He shrugged. "Sure, but I need you to answer my question."

171

Continuing her walk, Denefe passed him while she weighed her options. She couldn't really tell him the truth. There were people in the future who could be hurt. She said, "Didn't you hear what I just said? You lie to me, to everyone, and you seem to spend great amounts of time alone. Doesn't that sound suspicious to you?"

Falling in beside her, he asked. "The Hallen connection?"

"Who else could it be? He's the only one who's military." She tried her best to make it sound as if it were common knowledge. A dubious expression crossed his face and then disappeared, but he didn't deny it.

She continued, "I'm serious, though, about what I said. We're brother and sister. We need to stop bickering and start acting like we're important to each other, because I think we are. I know you're important to me and I want to get to know you better." It surprised her that she meant it.

"Okay, but I still can't let you leave here."

"Fair enough. I still can't let you keep me here. We're just going to have to agree to disagree on that point."

He smiled. "We can do that. Do you know you have leaves all over you?"

Chapter 42
Love By Any Other Name

Denefe spent the morning with Torenz. He trailed her to breakfast and then exercised with her and Jileah. Somehow, the three of them managed to turn it into a competition until Denefe had to beg off because of the remaining weakness in her limbs and belly. In truth, she felt fine, worn out like an old rag, but fine. She just really needed time to adjust to having a brother. When she wasn't suspicious of him, she found she actually liked him.

He seemed intent on staying with her, so she let him walk her to her quarters.

"We should do this again tomorrow," he said. "I had a great time."

"Or we could go bowling. Or go to a baseball game. Or even *play* in a baseball game. Oh, wait. We can't. That's right."

He frowned, white brows underscoring the harsh creases in his forehead. "Do you have to spoil it?"

"Torenz, I realize you grew up here, so you may not be aware, but there's a whole world out there and it's filled with things to do. Things for you to explore just because you can."

His gaze roamed and then he focused back on her. "Maybe tomorrow you'll be in a better mood." He pivoted on his heel and walked away.

Great! Now she put him back on his guard. She sent after him, *"I'm sorry. I just miss everyone and everything so much. I'll be better tomorrow. Promise."*

"I'll hold you to that."

"Deal." She continued to her quarters and then flopped onto her bed without getting undressed. Nothing had ever felt so good in her whole life. Curling into the scrumptiousness of her blankets, she let herself drift away.

* * * *

It was late afternoon when Denefe felt a jab at her consciousness. Confused, she fluttered her eyes open and gazed around the dim light in her room. No one.

She reached for Torenz and found him sleeping.

In her mind, she asked, *"Who is it?"*

"It's me," came Ardense's strong voice.

"It's night there. I thought you didn't like talking at this time." She didn't really try to hide the sarcasm that flowed through her words.

He either didn't notice, which was unlikely, or he chose to ignore it. *"Denefe, we need to talk."*

She sighed. There was no getting away from it. She might as well let him have his say so he'd leave her alone. *"In case you haven't noticed, talking is all we have anymore."*

"I'm not sure what I said that upset you so much." He waited.

She just wanted out of the conversation and, by his beginning, this threatened to be a long one. *"Nothing. It was nothing at all. I'm just in a bad mood."*

"Denefe, I know you well enough to see when I've

174

hurt you. Please tell me."

She relented. What did it matter now? *"You said you'll have to think about what I asked. This from the man who said he'd love me forever?"*

"So now you think I don't love you."

"No. I don't. I think you love my abilities or my looks."

"I don't know what to say to make you understand. I love you. I really do. I would follow you anywhere if I knew you loved me too. You've never said it and you make plans that don't include me. What am I supposed to believe? Should I give up everything for a woman who doesn't necessarily love me? What kind of fool would I be?"

So it was her fault then. No surprise there. Kaleen's words came back to haunt her, *Don't mess this one up. You always do.* Did she want to spend the rest of her life with Ardense? Yes. Absolutely. She wanted to tell him, but what came out was quite different. *"I'm scared."*

"I know that. It's why I haven't given up on you yet. For the life of me, I can't figure out what frightens you so much."

Denefe swallowed. In for a dime, in for a dollar. Might as well confess it all. *"I'm scared you'll leave me, because you love me for some reason other than just me."*

"That doesn't make sense. You're sure I'll leave, so you withhold the one thing I need to hear to make me stay? And because I love you for some other obscure reason, then I won't stay anyway?"

Her mouth went dry. That was it in a nutshell. *"Yes."*

"Do you know how crazy that sounds? How crazy you sound?"

Denefe's anger built. She'd opened her heart to him. Told him her deepest fear, and he'd made fun of it. She

175

said nothing, trying to swallow her feelings.

After a moment, Ardense said, *"I'm not the guy who'd do that. You know that, right?"*

Like a snap of her fingers, her anger dissipated. So did her fear. No longer was she one of the strongest telepaths on record. No longer was she a commodity owned by GlobeX. She was just Denefe, loved by Ardense. She nodded as she answered. *"I know."*

After another long pause, he asked. *"Do you love me?"*

She teared up and whispered the words even as she said them in her mind. *"Yes. I love you."*

Chapter 43
Silenced

Nine and a half days. It had been nine and a half days since her sister had been snatched by the sidewinder. It felt like an eternity. Kaleen glanced at Ardense. His gaze was locked on the path he flew through the rainforest. The trees outside the skimmer flipped by them at an impressive speed. Green after green after green. It was dim there. The morning light couldn't even make it through the dense canopy overhead.

"Did Cardenza say why he was coming here?"

He shrugged, but didn't take his gaze off their target path. "He said he'd discovered something urgent and he wanted us to meet him at the airport."

She studied him. For two days, the corners of his mouth had been habitually downturned, but not today. "You and Denefe make up? You look happier."

"Huh?" Now he looked at her, clear brown eyes opened wide in surprise, the skimmer slowing. After a moment, he turned back toward the task of flying, and they picked up speed again. "Yeah. We made up last night."

"So, you're going to let Bridger remove your microchip?"

His face turned stormy and he spoke carefully. "No. Not yet. If she's trapped in the past permanently, then I want to be with her. If what you and Bridger say is true, I can't go if I have no chip."

Kaleen sighed. It was exactly what she'd been thinking too. It would be heartbreaking to leave Bridger, but there was no way she could live without her twin. "I'll go with you."

"Did you tell Bridger your plan?"

"No."

"Don't you think he should know you might go to the past to live with Denefe?"

When she didn't answer, he straightened, and said, "You and your sister sure are hard on your men."

Her jaw dropped open and her face flamed in anger. She spat, "He's not my man."

He looked her straight on, eyebrows raised. "Sorry. I guess I was wrong."

Slowly, Kaleen nodded. After a moment of silence in which Ardense returned to studying the path in front of them, she said, "Of course, the best option is to bring her home."

"Right." He nodded.

Silence returned to the skimmer. Ardense flew, and Kaleen watched the dense rainforest roll on, becoming thinner as they neared civilization, sunlight breaking through to mark the ground. Eventually, the green of trees and moss gave way completely to the gray of buildings. As they neared the airport, the green of grass became the black of tarmac and parking lots.

They arrived late. Cardenza was already walking out of the gate, wearing a thick-browed frown. As they approached, he caught sight of them, smiled, and lifted a wave. Around him, the crowd streamed past, most people headed in individual directions, ignoring the man who now brought his hand sharply to his left temple. Even as he fell to his knees, people sidestepped him and continued on. It wasn't until he yelled like a wild animal that they slowed.

His head exploded.

Ardense launched out of the skimmer without even stopping it first. Kaleen lunged across the seats and jammed the craft into park amid the sound of grinding gears and whining air engines. By the time she joined him on the sidewalk, she had to push through a large group of gawkers who surrounded Cardenza.

What she saw when she looked down on him made her shudder. His face was barely recognizable, one intact eye staring vacantly at her. Over half of his head was completely gone. The memory of Staphershire's injury superimposed over Cardenza's. Same injury, same place.

Ardense rifled through Cardenza's pockets. He pulled something out of the shirt pocket, glanced at it, and abruptly stood, pulling Kaleen out of the crowd toward the skimmer.

Chapter 44
Cardenza

Denefe napped, dreaming of Ardense. Once she woke up, almost four hours later, her stomach growled like a wild animal. Even though she now had a clock on her comm, she still felt disjointed, as if she were perpetually in night. How did people live like that?

She cleaned up and then headed to the dining room where she found herself to be the only person present. That was what she got for sleeping through supper.

She was halfway through a plate of fish and chips, or something made to taste and look like it, when Kaleen called her.

"Denefe." She sounded strained.

"Hey, you."

"I have some bad news."

Denefe checked on Torenz. It was daylight, and he was back to his listening game. To Kaleen, she began *"Do you remember the time—"*

"Cardenza's dead," Kaleen choked out.

"What? How?" She felt as if she'd just been punched in the jaw.

"He was coming to visit. Apparently, someone

waited for him at the airport and bashed in his head."

The biggest question was "Why?" but she knew the answer already—because he'd found something Hallen wanted kept secret.

Kaleen continued. *"I just wanted you to know. You two weren't very close, but you worked for him."* She paused. *"You started to say something? 'Do you remember...', or something like that."*

Even through the stunned fog, Denefe understood that Kaleen had more to tell, but only in code. She flicked on her comm so she could type the conversation. She wouldn't dwell on the message right now, not with Torenz, or any other telepath, possibly—probably—listening. She just needed what Kaleen said, verbatim. She would think on it later when she was sure no one listened. Her job right now was just to respond to Kaleen, make it seem like a normal conversation.

"Do you remember I said you didn't have to stay up at night to contact me, that you could wake me any time you wanted?" No need to mention the blue dress at that point.

"Missing Cardenza kept me up all night. It's just horrible." Kaleen's thought voice broke.

"I guess it's rough on you too." More than a code, Denefe meant it.

"It's killed my appetite."

"Make sure you eat, even though you're not hungry. You don't need to get sick."

"I'll chipper up eventually."

"I know you will." She nodded, as if her sister could see it.

"The message of his death took me by surprise."

"He was too young."

"Call Ardense. It'll help him quit being so upset too." Kaleen was finished, as she showed by her usage of the word quit, but Denefe had a message for her as

181

well.

"*I will. Mine will be there a little bit longer, I think.*"

"*I understand that.*" Good, she got it. Sometimes, the word "mine" got lost in the whole secret code thing.

Denefe continued, "*I found that out the last time someone I knew died.*"

Now it was Kaleen's turn to make the coded sentences seem normal. She responded, "*It's different for everybody.*"

"*His exit from life stuns me.*" This was one of the awkward sentences that came from making an impromptu code. Someone listening would question it, but there was nothing she could do. Her second word had to be "exit."

"*I'm sorry. We all exit one way or another.*"

"*Thanks, but as you said, we weren't close.*"

"*Still hurts, though.*" More than just a response, Kaleen's telepathic voice was thick with the hurt of losing someone she'd known. As far as Denefe knew, no one close to them had ever died. That man had gotten her out of jail.

"*The problems we had with those above us might be moot now. Maybe we won't have to quit our jobs anymore.*" Her message, "found exit but problems," was done.

"*There is that.*" Kaleen's response wasn't a question. She got the message.

Quiet filled the void between them. Each seeking comfort in the presence of the other. Denefe wanted to hug her sister close, to console her. Finally, she just said, "*Thanks for the news.*"

"*Take care of yourself.*" Kaleen was gone.

Denefe turned off her comm and stared at her meal, not hungry. She had to eat, she'd told Kaleen to, but how could she? Cardenza was dead.

Finally, she put her still-full plate into the dispenser and then went back to her quarters. In disjointed bits and snatches throughout the evening, she figured out the code sentences Kaleen had said—Cardenza killed chipper-chip-message Ardense.

It was the microchip that had killed Cardenza, and Starry. Someone definitely wasn't happy. She, Kaleen, and Ardense all still had chips in their heads too. How much danger were they in?

Ardense had a message for her. From Cardenza?

Chapter 45
Last Message

In the dark of night, Denefe sat on her bed and stared at Ardense's now decoded message. She was right, it had been from Cardenza. It had taken him nearly an hour to deliver it, via some kind of alternate code. It turned out he used an alternating keyword system that she was able break. Still, it took yet another couple of hours for her to decipher it in bits and snatches into one short sentence.

Cardenza investigation rift irreparable degrading others spawning sidewinders everywhere must destroy from Denefe location get people out east arm.

She couldn't believe what she'd read. The dual bite of shock from the death of Cardenza, and now a final message from him, coursed through her like electricity. According to him, she had to destroy the rift and get all eighteen people safely across the desert and back into the future. How was she going to do that?

The end of the sentence was a bit cryptic. East Arm...? Was she supposed to go east? To a city that had Arm in it?

She stared at her parents' photo. Slowly, it came to her. The last bit was from Ardense. He knew she was familiar with only a few locations in Egypt. Armana, where Staphershire had been stationed and snatched from, was one of those.

First things first. Eighteen people across the desert. Very few of them would be able to stand the trek. She headed to the shuttle cart storage area. As far as she knew, they were the only other transportation for the facility. There, she inspected the fuel cells on the small machines. Most of them were viable, but a few weren't. Those would be left behind. She was glad to see the tiny hitch beneath the chassis of each. They'd be simple to link together and join to the skimmer.

All she needed now was some connector cables and tools. The area she was in was sparse and she didn't remember seeing much of any equipment in the bay behind the wall either. Where would she get the tools she needed to disconnect and reconnect the fuel cells?

Frowning, she walked toward the secret lab and skimmer. As she passed Jileah's locked office, she remembered seeing a pair of medical clamps on a table last time she'd exercised. Maybe those would work as tools. She'd have to check it out in the morning.

Once she stepped through the wall and entered the hidden bay, she saw a difference immediately. After her test drive, she'd carefully parked right back where she'd found the skimmer, just a little left from dead center of the outer door. Now, it stood distinctly to the right of the door.

Torenz? Or did he have an accomplice?

In a panic, she rushed to the machine, turned it on, and settled in for another test drive. The gauges showed fine and it still handled well. Perhaps it had just been maintained.

Or there could be another reason it had been moved. She narrowed her eyes at the DNA lock on the door. Was she mistaken, or did it look new? She climbed out of the shuttle and went to investigate. Again, she scuffed her hands in grime and then pressed her thumb onto the lock. Instead of flashing green on the second try, as before, it took five more attempts and, in fact, ended up being the index finger on her other hand that triggered it to open. Behind the door was the same desert air as before.

It occurred to her that she still hadn't checked the tunnel. She needed to ensure there were no obstructions. She flicked on her comm and walked the length of it, arriving at the opening before she realized it. The vista opened before her, the light from a quarter moon reflecting dully from the light-colored sand.

Denefe turned around and around, looking for east. Other than the tunnel entrance concealed beneath a rock overhang, there were no landmarks of any kind. She was glad she had her comm to act as a compass.

The sky was magnificent, though. Millions of stars glinted in the depths of it, like glitter on black velvet. She sighed. If she wasn't trapped in the past, away from everyone she loved, she'd be happy staring at that night sky for the rest of her life. Jerking her gaze from the beauty above, she took a closer inspection of the dunes. Storms drove them into different shapes and sizes. Tiny ridges echoed across the sand, like rings from something thrown into a pond. It made the dunes look alive, and powerful.

After one last look at the sky, she returned down the tunnel and then closed the door again, carefully wiping the dirt from the new DNA lock. Had Torenz figured out she'd been there? Or was he just taking precautions?

Returning to the skimmer, she inspected the skin mountings, her original reason for coming. If they were going to weigh the skimmer down with people and the shuttle carts tied behind, it had to take them the distance. She'd have to strip the machine as much as she could.

The skin looked fairly simple to remove. Basically, they'd be flying just a skeleton with a motor. She'd like to do something to make it more aerodynamic. A pointed nose and a scoop on the back wouldn't hurt.

Her biggest problem would be how to protect the air intake more than it was currently. Everything she thought of would take time to build.

She was going to have to fashion some kind of snowshoes for those who had to trek across the sand on foot. Perhaps she could punch holes into some of the metal skin to tie to their feet.

Like it or not, she needed help.

Chapter 46
An Accomplice

"Denefe." Jileah leaned close. "Where are you? You've been so distracted this morning."

Denefe shrugged. "I'm sorry. I'm just not sleeping well." Or at all, she thought. Between her nocturnal activity and trying to retain a semblance of a normal-ish daytime life, she was exhausted. She shoved her breakfast to the side.

"I can give you something for that. I have this great little chamomile blend that'll knock you right out." She sat back proudly and smiled.

Denefe smiled in spite of herself. The truth was, besides being worn out physically and emotionally, she was worried. How was she supposed to get a skimmer ready to haul all the people stationed there? How could she convince them to go if she couldn't talk to them about it until the last minute? She'd have to trust Jileah…carefully.

"I'm anxious too. I want to get home again. It seems odd to me that most people here are happy in the past."

"I'd say that's true. These people are experts in their fields. They've come here to study the anomaly."

"It's damaged. What if it continues to splinter?

What if it gets so bad it becomes unsafe to be around? Or it implodes and disappears entirely? What then?"

The nurse smiled. "Not everyone works with the anomaly directly. Actually, since it's been locked up, no one does. Quite a few work with barometrics and spectral readings, past and present. They feel they'll be able to better predict where the sidewinders are going to hit. They don't need the anomaly. If it ceased to exist, they'd still have work to do here."

"They'd be trapped here forever."

"That was the ticket we all bought. Well, except you and Torenz. He was too young to choose."

"What about you? You were brought here as a kid too. You didn't get to choose. Do you want to stay?"

A wistful look settled on Jileah's face. "Me? I still remember what it was like in the future world. I don't suppose it would matter what I, or anyone, would want. If that rift goes, we're all trapped here."

It was as good an opening as Denefe was likely to get. "So, if I can find a way home, do you want to come with me?" She watched her friend closely.

Jileah laughed and snapped her fingers. "As fast as that. I'd even race you to the finish line." She hesitated and then leaned in close, whispering, "That's it, isn't it? It's what's been bugging you. You think you've found it."

Denefe gave a single nod.

The nurse was speechless a moment. She continued, "What you said about the anomaly, is that what your friends in the future say?"

Denefe softly said, "Normally, I'd move into telepathic range, but Torenz has been listening in on my thoughts too much lately. We can't risk him hearing us." Still, she would listen to Jileah's thoughts, though it gave her more than a small pang of guilt. She needed to know if she could trust the nurse. It would help her to

189

pinpoint any hesitancy, hardness, or dislike by how her friend phrased herself or practiced a sentence before she spoke. It was hard work, because a telepath couldn't speak and read at the same time. She'd have to bounce back and forth, but make the conversation appear normal.

Jileah asked, "Why the secrecy?"

"Because Torenz lies. As do his employers. We can't trust him, yet."

"He's lied to me on occasion too. Why would he lie about something so dangerous and important like the rift?" Jileah's whispered words were guarded, but Denefe saw her thoughts were straightforward.

"Truthfully, he may not know." She knew the conversation she'd overheard from behind the wall meant that he did. "He knows we're not in the Gobi Desert."

"Not in…? Then, where are we?" Jileah frowned.

"The Egyptian. There's another rift a day's travel from here."

The nurse's face paled. She stared at Denefe for a moment, speechless. Her mind was a whirlwind with no distinct thoughts. It was plain Jileah hadn't known the truth. Denefe left her mind, guilt flowing through her like a river. Now she knew she could trust the nurse.

Abruptly, Jileah stood. "Why are we waiting? Let's go."

Denefe pulled her friend back to her seat. She whispered, "We can't leave yet because the rift is dangerous. It's going to disintegrate soon. We don't know how bad it will be when that happens, so we can't leave anyone behind. We need a way to get them out. Torenz might try to stop us."

"Why? Why would he do that?"

"It's his job. He works for the military in the future. He may or may not take their side in this, but we can't

190

risk letting him know what's going on until the last minute. Then, if he wants to join us, we'll have room. If he tries to stop us, we'll be ready."

Jileah licked her lips. "How soon is this going to happen? How much time do we have before the anomaly breaks down completely?"

"Soon. I need help getting everything ready."

The nurse nodded. "What do you want me to do?"

"Don't let on to anyone about our plans or even that we have a way home. Remember, speaking to my brother would be a bad thing. We'll need a few items and as many fuel cells as you can muster."

Jileah frowned. "Fuel cells?"

"You know, from the lab equipment and things like that."

"Oh, got it." Jileah got up and left the dining room.

Meanwhile, Denefe thought, the biggest problem would be to convince Torenz to come with them.

Chapter 47
Alone

Torenz stared at the notepad on his desk in the hidden lab. Beside him, the violet wormhole buzzed and angry tingles nipped his skin. It had been that way for a while, and that notepad wasn't where he'd left it.

Denefe had been there.

He had no idea how she'd accessed the hidden bay and lab, but he was sure it was her.

Pivoting, Torenz walked slowly back to the bay, watching the floor, noting scuffs in the dust and a myriad of prints near the skimmer and the locked exit door. He was glad now that he'd taken the precaution to change the lock. Safe was better than sorry, as his mom used to say.

Thinking of his mom saddened him. He missed his parents. More now than ever. He'd never felt so alone.

True, he and Denefe were on better terms. They didn't spat as much anymore, but she spent the majority of time telling stories and reminiscing with Kaleen. He had no doubt some of it was code, like that bit about the blue dress, but Hallen's guys hadn't found a key for the rest, or if it even was code.

Torenz grimaced. Or maybe they had. They didn't

share things with him like before. They'd refused his every offer of help. In fact, since they'd decided to spy on him as well, they hadn't spoken to him much at all.

He had no idea what was happening.

He was going to find out.

Chapter 48
Out of Time

For the next two days, Denefe spent every spare moment she could with Torenz, showing him how important it was to have family. Yet, no matter how much she tried, she often found him in her mind, listening to her thoughts. He'd promised a zillion times to stop, but he never did. It was possible he knew no other way to behave. After all, he'd been raised to be a spy.

In the darkness of night, Ardense told her another story about the puppy, outlining in code how to make a bomb. Denefe would fasten a small fuel cell to her comm and hide it near the rift. The comm would count down and then superheat the fuel cell, causing it to explode and thereby destroying the rift. What happened after that was anybody's guess, though it wouldn't be worse than the amount of sidewinders the rift was currently producing. Still, she hated the waste of a fuel cell.

As usual, hearing her boyfriend's warm telepathic voice in her mind made her heart seize with longing for home.

She asked, *"How is everyone?"*

"We're good. I can't say that for the rest of the

world, though. *We're starting to see more and more sidewinders. In New York, a rift opened up and snatched a bus load of people and a group of five at the bus stop. Some of them haven't been found yet, but the rest were found three days later when they appeared in six different locations around the world. Most were burned beyond casual recognition. Another opened in Paris near the Eiffel Tower and nearly swallowed a tourist family with their baby. In Moscow, another family just disappeared from their house in a small sidewinder. All this, plus more, in the last twelve hours.*"

His telepathic "voice" dropped a timbre. *"I can't wait to get you in my arms again."*

"That sounds wonderful."

They were silent a moment, basking in their thoughts of being together again.

"Well," she thought. *"I suppose I should get to sleep."*

"I'll talk to you tomorrow night."

"Yes, you will. Love you." It amazed her, now that the initial admission had been made, how easy those words rolled off her tongue. As if they belonged on her lips, being said in every sentence.

"Love you too."

After he left her mind, the silence was deafening. She walked toward the hidden bay and the rift and checked on Torenz's thoughts. He was quiet. Really, really quiet. Listening? She tried a test, but received no response. She stopped and glanced around her. What was he up to? After waiting for a moment and seeing no one near, nor reading a change in her brother, she continued toward her destination. The plans were set and everything was in motion. No matter what happened now, she and those going with her had to continue on. Torenz or no.

Once Denefe arrived at the magic disappearing

195

wall, she turned on her comm and executed the program. She smiled as the wall vanished.

"I've been trying to figure out how you do that," came Torenz's voice from behind her. "What does this make, your third trip into there?"

Denefe whirled to see her brother standing in the doorway to the lab. How could she have been so stupid? If she could school her thoughts, why didn't she expect him to learn how? She faced him square on. "Fifth, actually. Then, who's counting? Oh, that's right. It's you."

He nodded. "Whatever you're planning, which is obviously an escape in the skimmer, won't work." He stepped closer. "You're too far from the nearest anomaly, even with your modifications."

She must have looked as stunned as she felt, because he continued as he approached. "Oh, yes. I've noticed the quick release clips you tried to hide on the fenders." He held out his hand. Did he actually expect her to just hand over the comm? Her freedom?

She backed into the hidden lab, working the comm behind her back. Stale air surrounded her while rift spiders crawled across her. Her feet scuffed and echoed loudly.

Torenz said as he continued toward her, "I'm not sure how you tricked the DNA lock at the end, but I saw you've been down the tunnel too. Did you enjoy your view of the desert? You've seen how desolate it is out there. You *know* you can't make the distance. Give me the comm."

It sounded as if he, at least, didn't know about the bomb or the scientists leaving with her. She whipped the comm around in front of her and pointed it at the wall, pressing the execute button at the same time. The wall reappeared between them, solidly in place. She kept her thumb on the execute button, effectively jamming any signal he would send to bring the partition down again.

She leaned against the wall, knowing he could hear her. "News flash for you—I'm not staying here. Go with me. You know the rift is badly damaged. It's just a matter of time before it collapses. Then what will you do? Assuming it doesn't destroy the facility, you'll be trapped here forever. You won't be able to leave at all because *I'll* have the skimmer. Let's say you somehow manage to get out of here and across the desert, what then? Because when this rift goes, it'll take all of them with it. You'll be trapped in the past forever."

"I'm *already* trapped in the past." Anger rippled through his voice, making it come out as a growl.

"The difference is, right now you know you have a way out if needed. If that rift fails, you won't have that emergency exit just down the road and you'll know it every second of every day. You'll be trapped in this tiny underground base. It's a nifty vacation spot, but not really viable for a permanent home."

Torenz roared her name. "Denefe!" He was silent, except for his aggravated breathing.

She called Jileah. *"Wake up!"*

"Wha...Denefe?"

"I'm sorry for intruding, but I'm in trouble and I need your help. Torenz found out part of our plan and now I'm trapped behind the wall with the rift."

"What do you want me to do?"

"Wake everyone."

"I'm on it."

Denefe pivoted and ran to the skimmer. She needed to keep Torenz from informing his contact at Hallen's office about the planned escape. She entered her brother's mind and started speaking gobbledy-gook and fragmented sentences. It should confuse him, if not drown out any other telepathic conversation he had going on at the time. The skimmer looked okay from a distance, but as she neared, she saw the new welds added to keep the skin in place. She also noted the gel chains running from the frame to the floor, complete with some kind of lock she'd never seen before.

Denefe kept up her flood of babblings in Torenz's mind until she heard loud voices and scuffs on the other side of the wall.

She shot a short message to Ardense. *"Now."*

"Got it." The strength behind the thought filled her with confidence. She could do this. She could get all eighteen people to safety.

"Love you." It seemed inadequate for her feelings. She hesitated, wanting to say more, but not knowing what. How could she tell him how much he meant to her? She'd rather die than live without him any longer.

Chapter 49
Into the Desert

Jileah called from the lab on the other side of the wall. "It's all clear. You can come out now."

Denefe lifted her thumb off her comm, and the room opened to her. Torenz lay propped against a desk, unconscious, and with a swelling bruise over one temple. Regret burned a hole in her. He was her brother and yet he was her enemy.

Glancing at Jileah, she asked, "You've told everyone about the rift and that we're leaving?"

At her friend's nod, she motioned to the skimmer. "Get someone to cut those chains and remove the skin. We need to get it as light as possible. We also need some of these people to build snowshoes to help us through the sand when the skimmer fails."

Jileah's face paled. "So you don't think we'll make it."

"Most of the way, yes, but there will be a march at the end. How far depends on how light we can make the skimmer. Send a bunch of people to bring the shuttle carts."

Within two hours, the skimmer resembled a giant mechanical duck with its ducklings lined up behind it. Denefe assigned two scientists to guard duty. Their sole job was to keep Torenz medically knocked out until they were far enough from the rift so he couldn't contact anyone.

She opened the exit to the desert and the dark coolness of the dry night filled the tunnel and bay. As the procession passed through the exit, she counted— eleven scientists, five sundry support workers, one holistic healer, one traitor, and herself. The moon was full and the sand dunes looked like giant waves in an ocean that her group sailed upon, Jileah's comm lighting the way. By the time she lost sight of them over a giant of a dune, they were a good mile away.

Going back into the facility, she set her homemade time bomb in place at the base of the rift.

Her father's journal had been discovered while the skimmer crew had stripped the shuttle carts. Denefe debated taking it, but in the end, she reasoned it didn't weigh much so she snatched it up and tucked it into her shirt. She stepped out onto the sand, strapped on her snowshoes, and took off at an easy swinging jog after the slow-moving group.

It didn't take her long to catch them as she closed the gap. She urged them faster. "Come on! We've got to get to the other rift. Move!"

Jileah frowned at her and made room to run beside her. She asked, "What's the hurry?" Besides the nurse, there were four others in athletic enough shape to make the trek on foot. The rest would take turns trekking and riding in the carts.

"I don't want this getting around, but in ten hours the military is shutting the rift down rather than let it disintegrate on its own. They've decided it's safer that way." A small lie, but it was close to the truth.

"We need to be on the other side by then."

Denefe nodded. "This trip is supposed to take only seven and a half hours. Let's see if we can mush this

200

group a bit faster. It's cool tonight so the exercise will warm everyone."

"It would help if Torenz wasn't dead weight riding. Besides you, he's probably the most fit of all of us."

"We can't trust him. If he makes me angry enough, then we can't trust me." She hated that it was true. She might leave him in the middle of the desert.

"I think, then, that it's better he remains unconscious."

"For now. When we reach a safe place, I'll wake him and he can run."

Denefe set a hard pace, pushing those on foot to keep up with her and the skimmers. As the fuel cells spent in the shuttle carts, she cut them loose from the train and let them drift away. Truthfully, she thought more than once about abandoning her brother in one of those. She could just let it list in the desert and all her problems, well, most of them, would be solved. Her hesitation unnerved her. Was she seriously considering it?

She marched the group for almost four hours. Twice she called for a break. Dawn was stretching across the sandy dunes when Denefe called for the third break and thought to check on Torenz. Already, the warmth of the upcoming day battled away the chill of the night. They'd have to hurry or they'd be running in the heat.

"How is he?" she asked the scientist, Roy something. Names were hard for her, especially with people she never interacted with.

"Sleeping like a baby." He beamed at her.

"Did you give him another tranquilizer?" She leaned close to her brother, peering at his face, watching his eyelids. She entered his mind, but found it silent, as if asleep...or faking it.

"We haven't needed it. The first one seems to have taken him for quite a ride."

Torenz's eyelids rested peacefully closed. He seemed to be asleep, and yet... She blew a puff of air against his eyes. Though they didn't open, a small wrinkle appeared in the upper crease of each. He overrode his natural instinct and was instead pressing his eyes shut.

"Faker," she whispered.

Torenz's eyes shot open, anger clear across their brown depths. He made no attempt to keep his voice low. "You're dead. Do you know that?"

She straightened and smiled sweetly. "I have no doubt they'll try. You need to worry about what they'll do to *you* after letting me take control of the facility."

It satisfied her to see the shock that ripped across the face that was so much like her own. She considered. They were by far too distant from any rift for him to reach through to Hallen. She patted the shuttle. "Time for you to get out and run like a big boy."

In a fit of starting and stopping, he slowly climbed out and pulled himself erect beside her. His mouth was a bitter twist of anger, but he put on the snowshoes she threw at his feet. An exhausted scientist took his place in the cart. Turning, she motioned for the train to get moving again. They were on schedule, but just. She wanted enough extra time to handle any complications that might arise.

Chapter 50
Proof

Kaleen squirmed, trying to find a comfortable position. The unyielding chairs she and Ardense sat in lined the wall of a long, busy hallway filled with moving military people. On the other side of the hall was a frosted windowpane door with the letter "B" stenciled on the glass. No name, just "B."

Ardense leaned into her and spoke in a low voice. "Are you sure we can trust this guy?"

She barely heard him over the noise, but she shrugged. She'd been hearing and asking that same question a lot lately. "Cardenza did."

Truthfully, she didn't know and that bothered her. It also bothered her that, because of this whole mess, Ardense couldn't ask her that private of a question telepathically. It felt as if they'd become suddenly naked to the rest of the world, having to voice everything.

Office door "B" opened, and a stout dark man beckoned to them.

Kaleen crossed the hallway, dodging between oncoming traffic, and entered the office, Ardense right behind her. The man, Lieutenant Garza, or so his nameplate read, motioned to the two chairs facing his meticulous desk, while he seated himself behind. A shaded window on the side wall let in enough sunlight to shadow half his face, even with the overhead lights.

She smiled at the lieutenant. "I understand you knew Maurice Cardenza."

"I did. He was a good friend." He hesitated, a heavy sadness washing across his face, then he said, "We were in the military together. I can't tell you how many times we saved each other's lives."

Ardense said, "We learned to trust him, and he trusted you."

When Garza nodded, Kaleen moved to the edge of her seat, leaning into the desk. "We know that GlobeX is military-run. You were military. You understand our concern?"

He frowned at her. "The military only ensures that the private corporation, GlobeX, obeys the Temporal Accord. We have no hand in the operation of the company. I can assure you, I'd know if it was otherwise."

She smirked. "I don't believe you. Bade Hallen arrested me. He can only do that if he's military." She settled against the back of her chair, arms crossed, waiting to hear his excuse.

A spark came alive in Garza's eyes. "I promise you, GlobeX isn't military. Bade Hallen, however, is a person of interest." He picked up his comm and worked his fingers across the device. Then he handed it to her.

She leaned toward Ardense with it, letting him read at the same time. After a moment, she lifted her gaze, and said, "It says here that you suspect he's German military."

Ardense chimed in, "From 1940?" He took the comm completely from her now, continuing to read the report.

Garza said, "He was told about the wormhole. He came across, worked himself into a key position, and has been manipulating the timeline in the past to assist Nazi Germany ever since."

Ardense handed the comm back. "Why hasn't he been stopped?"

"Persecuting a telepath or someone involved in a telepathic crime requires multiple personal testimonies and, as of yet, we've been unable to define anyone in his operation. Basically, we have nothing for the courts."

Now Kaleen frowned. "Then, how do you know he's this Nazi soldier?"

"We have the man who helped him across. His testimony only makes the crime one of misusing the wormholes, a deportable offense. By manipulating the timeline, Hallen's committed some very serious crimes. We want him accountable."

Satisfied they could trust Garza, she nodded at Ardense.

He produced the documents he'd taken from Cardenza's pocket. "We believe Cardenza was killed because of what he found. It's on paper because, when telepathic spies are involved, everything must be spoken and written. Not thought on like you would when typing an electronic document."

Garza reached for the papers, unfolding them as he spoke. "I understand that. Murder would be easier to prove and it could be the crowbar that breaks open Hallen's operation. A deal could then be offered to those arrested, that the first person who talks gets a lesser charge."

Kaleen waited, watching the military man read his friend's notes. His lips moved as he read. After he finished, he leaned back in his chair, staring at the documents.

She said, "We believe Staphershire, the time jumper stationed in Egypt, was killed for discovering a hidden base in the past, the same thing Cardenza uncovered, and the same place Denefe is being held captive."

Ardense handed across another wad of folded papers from his pocket. "These are transcribed notes and testimonies that Starry collected."

Garza shook his head. "The report said Staphershire was killed as a result of the sidewinder." He skimmed the new pages.

While he read, Kaleen continued. "I'm the one who found him. I had a chance to inspect him before he was taken. The damage to his head was consistent with the detonation of this." She pulled out Starry's microchip and held it in her palm. "It was also consistent with what happened to Cardenza. It wasn't a mugging. We were there and saw it happen. His chip detonated."

Garza reached across the desk and plucked the chip from Kaleen's hand. He held it up between his thumb and forefinger, studying it. "This might be exactly what we need."

Chapter 51
Conflicted

Torenz eyed Denefe. She ran to the left of the line, constantly shifting her gaze to watch the horizon and the group of fugitives. Each time her gaze rested on him, her shoulders drooped and her face saddened. Then she moved her attention elsewhere.

He pondered this for a while. Could it be that she was sincere in her statements of affection for him? Not just tricking him to get free?

Was it something he could use against her? If he stopped her, he'd get back in Hallen's good graces.

It brought a pang of guilt with it, because he'd become fond of her. She was his sister and so like their parents. She was part of his family, part of him.

A burn of an ulcer wormed its way into his stomach.

Chapter 52
Decision Time

Denefe's people were slowing. As the sun lifted high in the sky and the heat rose, the energy in her little group wound down. A sand storm had passed through there recently and the soft grains underfoot sucked at their snowshoes. It clogged the motors of the vehicles. Already, she'd had to abandon one of the little shuttle carts ahead of schedule. That was something she hadn't counted on, not to this degree, at least. She figured they were running a good half an hour behind schedule.

She called Jileah. "We're going to have to pick up the pace."

The big nurse nodded grimly. Grime covered her face and scored her neck in lines. "I'll take the front."

Denefe eyed her string of mechanical conveyances. The individual carts wandered back and forth at the ends of their tethers, making the line of them look less like ducks and more like a snake. The last cart rocked back and forth in imitation of a boat trying to swamp. "I was thinking of dumping that last cart. The cell's almost shot and it's starting to waddle."

"What about who's riding in it? Where will they go? There aren't enough snowshoes."

"They'll just have to move into another or walk. I'll

give up my shoes if necessary." She'd make sure Torenz didn't have any either. She eyed her brother and caught him watching her. The moment he noticed her attention, he jerked his gaze away, scowling. She'd need to speak with him before they went too much farther. It was a task she didn't relish.

Jileah's face was still knit into a frown. "I think it'll slow us way down."

Denefe returned to the current conversation and pointed at the offending cart. "Or it could speed us up. The tow chain is as tight as a guitar string."

Jileah shrugged. "You're the boss." She moved away.

Denefe nodded and stepped up to the cart, disconnecting it. The lead vehicles picked up speed, leaving it behind. "Everybody out. This one's done." She jerked the fuel cell out for use in the skimmer later. Three scientists unloaded and began the trek on foot. None looked too happy.

They'd started with the skimmer and five shuttle carts, the others being in too much disrepair. Now they were down to three—skimmer and two carts. There wouldn't be so many breaks for the walkers anymore. She had only taken one since dumping Torenz onto his feet. She'd planned on another, but that wasn't going to happen now.

After another forty-five minutes of travel, Denefe was still trying to figure out how to win the angry, brooding Torenz to her way of thinking. She'd learned he was as quick to anger as she was and as stubborn as Kaleen. Not a good combination. She needed to find the perfect words to convince him.

She glanced again at the horizon ahead of her. She should be able to glimpse the town, Armana, by now, but all she saw was a thin black line where the sky started. Frustrated, she sputtered her lips. Jileah trudged beside her, breathing heavy, and the rest strung out in a long line behind, Torenz in the middle.

The nurse nudged her and pointed to a line of dust in the sky to the right. That didn't look good.

Denefe climbed onto the nose of the skimmer, rocking it wildly, and shaded her eyes, partly from the sun, but also from the sand particles. The dust cloud followed a dark clump that looked to be on an intersect course with her group, maybe a good ninety minutes or more distant, but it could be closer or farther. In the desert, distances were deceiving. She ran through the possibilities in her mind. Her brother could only have contacted another telepath already in that time.

She turned to Torenz. Incredulous, she asked, "What did you do?"

A smirk crossed his face, but he didn't answer.

She jumped down and urged her group to move faster. The soft sand they'd been slogging through had steadily been working up to hard pack again. She dropped to the middle of the line and ran beside her brother.

"Do you know what it's like to really be alone?"

"You know that I do."

"No, I mean really alone. That rift is going to close. When it's gone, you won't even able to listen in on my and Kaleen's thoughts."

"There are other telepaths."

"Do they fill the space inside like we do? Are you as close to them as you are to me? To us? You told me about when you were a child and you felt like two-thirds of you was missing. You'll feel that all the time."

When he didn't answer, she knew she'd hit pay dirt. She remembered the silence after her and Kaleen's fights. She continued. *"I know what it's like to be that close to someone and suddenly lose that. We're family. No one else can fill that gap. Not these people, and not*

210

the other telepaths."

Hesitancy crept across his face, but still, he said nothing.

"I've told you from the beginning, I'm not staying. If I'm stuck here and if these people capture me, I'll make them sorry. In the end, they'll have no recourse but to let me go. Or kill me. You'll lose me. Either way, you'll have no connection to the future, so you'll lose Kaleen too. It'll be just you. Alone, with two-thirds of you gone."

She continued. *"I'll bet no one trusts you anymore, just because we're related. Do you really think that will change? You can work and work and work to prove yourself, but, in the end, you'll always be my brother to them—unable to be trusted, even if I fail. Even if it's you who stops me. Your time with these people is done. You know that's true."*

Now he looked at her, his white brows furrowed and his brown eyes clear with sudden understanding. *"I can't stop those who want you to stay here. I'm not that powerful in the hierarchy."*

"No, but you can stop working against us."

He gave a short nod. *"I'll do whatever you need."*

She breathed a sigh of relief. Until that moment, she hadn't realized how important he'd become to her. He was her brother, one-third of her. He was at least partly on her side now. Her heart surged. True, she couldn't trust him much, and she'd have to keep an eye on him, but hopefully he wouldn't actively work against her any longer. That was something.

Another twenty minutes passed, and Denefe was pleased to see a dot in front of them that began to resemble a town. She hopped on top of the skimmer again. The smudge on the cross trail was distinctly closer, even more than it should be. She could easily make out individual clusters. They couldn't be more than forty minutes out, coming fast. If her people were going to outpace them, she'd have to get them running. Time to cut some dead weight.

She jumped down and waved the group to a stop. "Okay. Let me tell you why we're all out here, in the middle of the desert. The rift has gotten dangerous. It's killing a lot of people. It's going to be destroyed. I had to get you far enough away in case something went wrong. The lab could be demolished. Sidewinders could fly out everywhere and, even though we're not safe from those out here, it's guaranteed we wouldn't survive them back there."

She held up her hand to forestall any comments, questions, or complaints. "It's decision time for you. I've been told many of you would prefer to stay here, in the past, even without the rift. It means you'll never return home again. All the rifts will be gone. You will become citizens of this timeline. You'll never get to know if anything you've done has been published or even recognized should you hide it for the future and that purpose. Worse, if the lab *is* destroyed, you'll have no equipment. Nor will any be coming from the future."

She pointed to the east and the oncoming bad guys. "We have a group of fast-moving individuals trying to reach us from this direction. I'm thinking whoever they are, they won't be a rescue party. They could be raiders."

At their startled faces, she added. "If you play your cards right, they most probably won't hurt you. You have bargaining power. We've left these shuttle carts scattered behind us, plus you'll have these two and the skimmer. You can barter them as you need. So, decide now—stay or go, but decide quickly. We have no time and we'll be moving fast. If you can't keep up, we won't wait for you and you'd be better off staying here. Those of you who are leaving, get moving."

The group sifted and thinned, leaving behind four scientists. Torenz moved on with the group going to Armana.

Denefe said to the small group staying, "Good luck." She ran to catch up with her smaller caravan of Jileah, Torenz, and twelve others. Most of them were fairly fit, but there was one who shouldn't be with them. She thought she remembered his name as Baker or something like that.

She pulled him aside. "Stay here. The pace we've got to keep is too much for you and we can't help."

He barked a laugh and appraised her with his eyes. "I'll take my chances with you."

Denefe shrugged and moved on. It would be his funeral. Her hope was that all the raiders would stay focused on the other group of scientists, but to her dismay, they split as well. Until that moment, she'd held a tiny hope they were just passersby. Watching them separate into two columns, her stomach pitched.

She kicked off her snowshoes and bolted. "Run! Run!" Jileah immediately followed Denefe's example and followed. Torenz bolted behind her. The rest of her people surmised the danger and joined them. One, not Baker, stopped and turned back to join the group staying behind.

It looked to be a close race whether they would reach the town or the advancing column would catch them first. Ahead of them, Armana grew steadily larger. Behind them, the time bomb was ticking.

Chapter 53
Run!

Denefe glanced behind at her little entourage. The majority of her people were clustered together, helping and encouraging each other. Behind them was Baker, flailing his arms across his body in an effort to make his legs move faster. Sweat stains covered his entire shirt and fresh sweat rolled down his face in sheets.

She gritted her teeth, veered to the side, and stopped. "Keep going!" she shouted at Jileah, who glanced at her with a questioning frown. Once the throng of scientists came abreast, she shouted "Faster! The raiders are gaining!" It was as if the sand suddenly boiled under their feet and the pace nearly doubled.

Baker finally came even with her, and she fell in beside him. "Stop sawing your arms across your body. It only uses energy faster. Move your arms straight forward like this." She demonstrated.

He tried it, exaggerating the move unnaturally. He grinned. "I knew you wouldn't leave me."

She snatched his arm and spun him around to face the oncoming raiders, who could now be seen to be riding animals of some kind, most probably camels. Horses would have gotten caught in the deep sands or broken through the crust and floundered, whereas the camels had wide, flat feet and traveled on top like a ship on the sea.

She pointed. "Do you see them?" She twisted him forward again and pointed to Armana. "You have to get to that town before those people catch you. Do you understand?"

He still grinned like an idiot. "I'm a behavioral scientist. I'm here to study people and the long-term effects of living in close proximity to an anomaly."

What was he babbling about? She gave him a rough shake. "Do you understand me?"

"Yes, I do." He started to run again, and Denefe kept pace with him. He concentrated on his arm movements, and then said, "I've studied you since you arrived and I knew you wouldn't leave me."

Studied her? When? How? She'd seen no one watching her, overtly or otherwise. It kinda felt creepy. She growled, "I still might. Now, stop talking, you're wasting energy." She increased her pace, forcing him faster, though he didn't appear to notice.

After running in silence for a few minutes, he nodded toward Torenz, who ran in front beside Jileah. "I've studied him for a long time now. I never liked him, nor trusted him. According to my studies, he'll betray you in the end."

She knew what Baker said was true, deep down inside. Torenz had spied on people, lied, kept secrets, and held everyone prisoner, but he was her brother. She had to give him a chance to straighten out his mistakes. Even if he didn't. That was all there was to it.

She pressed her lips together and increased the pace again. Baker was forced to focus on his running and he said no more. His breathing came more and more labored and raspy as they ran. She'd have to call a break, of sorts.

"Jileah. Can you and Torenz drop to a jog? Let's

215

give them a little break."

"Not a problem."

Immediately, as her brother and the nurse slowed, the cluster behind them stalled to a walk. When it became apparent the two were going faster than they, a few groaned and picked up the same pace, but the rest remained at a walk. Baker took his instruction from Denefe's pace and kept up a jog, though his face plainly showed his weariness.

Armana didn't seem to grow closer at all. She'd been wrong. The town was farther away than it looked. She glanced behind at the raiders. They were only about fifteen minutes away.

"Torenz. There's no way our group can get to the town before the raiders catch us."

Ahead, he stopped and watched the dust cloud grow nearer. *"It's the telepath from Hebenu. I've been trying to reason with him, but he won't listen. What if we all scatter? Some might be captured, but some would make it. Or we could split into small groups."*

"No, the best plan is to stay together, for now." Damn that Baker for reading her so well. She stopped beside her brother as Baker ran on. *"We could dig into the sand and hide."*

"These are desert people. They're used to those kinds of tricks."

"What would they not be used to? Think!"

"They'll most probably try to circle us. What would happen if we circled one of them instead? The leader, maybe?"

She nodded. It was a good idea, but they had a couple of problems with it. *"We don't really have enough people. Besides, can you see these scientists trying to bully someone?"*

His telepathic voice came grudgingly. *"No, I guess not."*

216

They lapsed into silence for a moment. Torenz said, *"It should be a simple matter to spook the camels, assuming they act like any other animal. I really don't know anything about them, but I seem to recall they don't have any natural predators."*

They began working on an idea.

Another ten minutes found her group at a full-out run again. The small slick on the horizon of Armana suddenly rose in front of them, but it wasn't quite close enough to save them from their followers.

The Hebenu telepath and his raiders were almost on top of them when a thin, reedy, telepathic voice broke into Denefe's thoughts. *"You won't make it. I have you."*

She neither slowed nor looked in his direction. She shouted at her group, "Keep going! No matter what, don't stop!"

The telepath laughed in her mind. *"I know your plans. I can see them."*

"Really? That's impressive if you can do that. Because from my experience, telepaths can only read what's being actively thought, not what's dormant. What makes it really spectacular is that I don't even know our plans. You must be part magician. Can I get your autograph?"

His "voice" was clipped, perhaps from embarrassment of his bluff being called. *"In Armana another telepath is waiting. He has instructions to stop you by any means necessary, including death. We both do."*

"That's nice. Can we discuss this later? I'm a little busy right now." The oncoming raiders were close enough they separated to circle Denefe's group of scientists. She and Torenz had to make their move now or never. She nodded to her brother. *"Now."*

Without stopping, she entered the mind of the camel

directly behind the leader. She'd never been inside an animal before. It felt wild and base. Very different from humans. She used the ancient Egyptian word for "stop" that Torenz had taught her. *"Khaloss."*

She jumped to the rider's mind. *"Khaloss,"* she said again. Beside her, Torenz did the same with others of the raider party. Still running, they moved from camel to rider to camel to rider through the eleven-member group behind the leader. The whole process took less than a minute. The telepath from Hebenu hadn't even noticed the chaos behind him yet.

For the first time, she and Torenz stopped and faced the telepath. Confusion filled his frown. No doubt he'd been following her thoughts but hadn't figured out yet what it meant or who it had been directed at. She sent the last command to his camel and, as the beast slowed to a stop, furious understanding burned across the telepath's face.

"Very clever, but it won't stop us for long."

"It doesn't need to. It'll be just long enough, I think, for us to reach Armana."

Chapter 54
Arrested

A few hours after meeting Lieutenant Garza, Kaleen and Ardense followed him and his men as they swarmed, quiet as death, into Bade Hallen's outer office. The helmet was suffocating her and she could barely move from the weight of the black protective gear. At least she didn't have to also contend with a gun.

She stumbled, but was caught by the uniformed officer next to her, who was at least twice her size and had fierce, restless eyes, as did all Garza's men. She wondered if that was a qualification, or if Garza's training put that into them.

As the group passed Hallen's assistant, the young man stood in protest, only to be shoved against the wall and handcuffed. A thick, gloved hand clamped over his mouth and he was hustled out the door in absolute silence.

Garza gripped the knob on Hallen's office door and scanned his men, receiving a nod from each. His gaze lit on Kaleen and Ardense and his mouth tightened into a thin line. He'd only agreed to bring them along because they were telepaths. It was apparent to Kaleen, he would have preferred someone telepathic *and* trained in military police tactics and weapons.

He twisted the knob and threw open the door. The group flowed into the office like a flood from a broken dam. The men scattered around the room, each to a different vantage point, all with weapons aimed at Bade Hallen. "Military police! Freeze!"

Hallen sat in a leather chair behind a giant mahogany desk. His uniform jacket was hung on the chair behind him and he held his hands stationary, six inches from his comm.

Garza and one of his men crossed the room in three easy strides and forcibly lifted the man from his seat. They pulled him to the side, in front of a tall window, flanked by giant wooden bookcases.

While he was searched and cuffed, one of the black uniformed men—Kaleen thought it was the same one who had kept her from falling—set down his weapon and searched the desk, violently pulling drawers open and rifling the contents. After he finished, he shook his head at the lieutenant.

Beside Kaleen, Ardense also shook his head. His voice came across in the speaker of her helmet. "I get nothing from Hallen."

Garza scowled.

Kaleen spoke into her microphone. "Let me try."

She entered his mind and found him silently singing a song to himself. It didn't surprise her that he knew how to beat a telepath. She, however, knew a few tricks of her own.

Building softly, she sang along with him, sending it to his mind, matching his thought pattern. After a moment, out of the blue, she sent the thought, *Kill. Microchip. Desk.*

Like a ringing bell, his mind made the automatic correction. *Comm.* Immediately, his face paled and the singing stopped.

She smiled. She'd beaten Bade Hallen.

She said to Garza, "The execute program is on his comm, not a remote or other device. Read the icons out loud."

The lieutenant nodded to the man behind the desk, who dropped into the leather chair and began reading. Hallen showed no response.

Garza's man stopped, and said, "That's all of them, except one that has no label. It's a smiley face."

Hallen's mind jumped in inadvertent connection. *Detonate.* His eyes widened momentarily, then his shoulders slumped and he dropped his gaze to the floor.

Kaleen said, "That's it. That's the trigger." She shuddered. Hallen was an evil man, using a smiley face to kill people.

Garza nodded. He stepped in front of his prisoner. "Bade Hallen, you're under arrest for a number of serious crimes, including, but not limited to, two counts of murder, espionage, numerous infractions of the Time Accord—"

Kaleen didn't hear the rest. Ardense pulled her out of the office, removing his helmet. "We can't stay. There's someplace we need to be."

Chapter 55
Armana

Denefe snatched Torenz's hand and bolted toward Armana in the morning heat. Her group was just entering the outskirts of town. She reached out in her mind for the telepath stationed there. He would be listening to her thoughts from the second she made contact with him, if he wasn't already. The Hebenu telepath would be following her thoughts too. He would assume Torenz was still working against her. She would have to be careful to keep thinking only what she wanted them to believe.

"Hello, telepath! This is Denefe Xia."

"What do you want? Where are you?"

"I have injured people and we need your help. We have raiders on our trail. Will you help me?"

"Where are you?"

"I am entering Armana from the east now. I'd like to meet alone with you first."

"There's a coffin-maker on the third street to the south. It's not a popular spot, and it's out of the way. It'll afford us some privacy."

"Fine." She cut her end of the telepathic link between them, carefully thinking of only their upcoming meeting. She and Torenz had a plan and, if he stuck with

it, they'd be fine.

They entered Armana and, after winding in and out of blind alleys, backtracking, and almost getting lost, they finally found a through street. Torenz split from her to take up his part in the plan, and she continued on. Midway down, she saw a coffin in front of a merchant shop. The telepath, the one who had been posted before Starry, leaned against the building, near the opening to a small alley.

Denefe had a hard time keeping herself from looking for her people as they skulked from building to building, Jileah in the lead. The desert telepath had followed her into the town and positioned his people around her. She concentrated on thinking how much she needed help, even though she didn't entirely trust anyone. She was desperate. People were injured and hurting.

As she approached, Starry's predecessor pushed himself off the wall, gesturing to the alley. "This is as private as I can make it."

She stopped and shook her head. "Not a chance I'm going down that alley."

"Look. You came here asking for my help. I appreciate that you don't trust me, but if you *want* my help, you have to at least come here and talk to me. I'm *not* talking over there." He raised his eyebrows, waiting for her response.

Still, Denefe clenched her teeth and let herself look around for signs of betrayal, pretending not to see the shapes of those hiding in the dark. One of those was supposed to be Torenz. She just hoped he stayed true to her.

She nodded and followed the telepath down the alley, settling against the wall, not a foot away from him. She spoke with a low voice. "You know we're from Definitive Headquarters, right? We all just want to get home again. During the crossing in the desert, we ran into a sand storm that flipped our skimmer. I have three injured people. We need help."

He nodded, his gaze on her. "It's okay. I can—" He whipped his head to the right, feigned fear clear on his face. "What was that sound?"

"I didn't hear anything."

"No? I'm sure I heard something. I think someone's here. Hurry." He gripped her arm and piloted her deeper into the alley, all the while taking quick glances behind him.

She almost laughed at the obviousness of his ploy, but she let herself be pushed deep into the dank recesses while she thought only on the possibility of someone intruding.

Once they'd gone into the alley far enough, he roughly pushed her against the side of the building, holding her there with his body. His voice dripped with loathing when he spoke. "You stupid fool. Do you think me, Hallen, or anyone for that matter, really care about you or those scientists?" He shouted for his partner from Hebenu.

Not for the first time was Denefe glad for her athletic training. She burst into a frenzy of punches, kicks, twists, and turns. More than once, she felt skin rip from her as she grazed against the stone building. The telepath hissed through his teeth as a few of her punches found his throat, inner thighs, and chest. She brought her elbow up and into his jaw, hearing the satisfying "clack" as his teeth slammed shut. The telepath worked to sweep her feet out from under her, but she countered, shoving her knee into the side of his.

Whirling to run, she saw she was trapped on that side by the Hebenu telepath and a few of his company. They wouldn't take her easily. She placed her feet and crouched low, glancing from side to side, alternately watching the two telepaths. Where was Torenz?

Two of the desert riders rushed her, and she dropped them with a sharp uppercut to the jaw of one and a heel in the groin of the other.

The entire group came at her then. She dispatched one with a roundhouse kick against his temple and followed with her other foot to punch another man.

She dodged outstretched arms and grasping hands and bolted down the first adjoining alley. She didn't think it would take her far, but since she was at the edge of Armana, it shouldn't be a dead end. Most towns, even in that time, had secondary and tertiary main streets with crisscrossing alleys. It was the nature of humans to want the easiest path. She hoped Armana wouldn't be any different. She turned out of her alley into another, and found it to be just that, a secondary main road. She grinned. Thank goodness for human nature! Still no sign of her brother, though. Where was he?

She began a mantra in her mind. *Get as far away as possible! Get as far away as possible! Get as far away as possible!* If she could just focus on just that, the telepath wouldn't read what little bit she knew of her group's plans. She'd been clear to Jileah not to divulge any of it to neither her nor Torenz. *Get as far away as possible! Get as far away as possible!*

The door of a house opened up to her, and she checked her pursuers. She had put some distance on them. They were just turning the corner. She skidded into the building, bolting up the stairs to the roof. The owner yelled angrily, shaking his fist at her. One of the women within the house screamed as Denefe flew past. *Get as far away as possible!*

She was on the roof. She crouched low to keep anyone from the telepaths' retinues from seeing her. Armana stretched before her and she spotted Starry's future house just in time to see the last of her group enter. *Get as far away as possible! Get as far away as possible!*

Her surmise about the shape of the town had been correct. It was long and narrow, with only one secondary street on each side. It looked as if it would be fairly easy once she got on the other side street to circle back to the rift. *Get as far away as possible! Get as far away as possible!*

Denefe looked down the main street again. Already, the two telepaths shouted instructions below. At least they'd focused on her and not on anyone else. They ordered a few of their people to follow her to the roof, but most were to circle the house. She ran for the edge of the wide, flat roof, heat reflecting from the white stones in waves. Hoping nothing was on the ground on the other side, she launched herself over and into the air.

Denefe tucked herself and, when she hit the ground, she let herself roll. The impact jarred her pretty badly, but she didn't think she'd injured herself. She shoved herself to her feet. Men came at her from both sides. Putting every ounce of energy into her legs, she sprinted for the telepath's house and the hidden time rift.

Where was Torenz? Had he, as Baker had warned, betrayed her?

Chapter 56
Home

Denefe threw herself through the door of Starry's future home, rift spiders crawling across her skin and a whole slew of angry men not too far behind. Rounding a corner, she plowed right into a hard, lean body. Instinctively, she launched into a tirade of upper cuts, jabs, and kicks.

"Whoa! Denefe, it's me!" Ardense backed away from her, brown eyes wild and hands up to ward off her attack. He had scrapes and cuts all over his face. One eye swelled shut. Those hadn't come from her.

She stared for a split second, then gripped his arm, rushing him toward the center of the house and the rift. "There are people behind me. Where's Torenz?"

"I knocked him out in a fight. Kaleen and I found your group surrounded by your brother and some men."

So, Torenz had betrayed her, after all.

They reached the *impluvium*, and Denefe asked, "Where's Kaleen?"

"Helping people through." He jerked his thumb toward the rift.

She opened her mouth to ask him more, but the sudden noise of voices close behind spurred them faster.

They bolted for the *ala* that hid the wormhole.

Kaleen stood by the side of the swirling anomaly, Torenz unconscious in a huddle at her feet. She was steadying the last person, Baker, as he stepped through. She looked up at Denefe and smiled, her nose crinkling. "There's a sight for sore eyes!"

"Hurry!" Denefe grabbed Torenz's arm. Ardense grabbed the other side and they propped her triplet between the three of them. Just as the Hebenu telepath, with Starry's predecessor right behind, entered the room, they stepped into the rift.

This time, she had no breakfast to turn her stomach into quivering spasms. Still, the pressure squeezed her unbearably, pinching her head into an ache. She wondered if it was the microchip reacting, if someone had pressed the detonator button. Now that she had found a way home, and was with her loved ones, someone was killing them. She would have laughed at their fate if she wasn't so scared. Only the pressure of Ardense's hand in hers kept her from full-out panic.

They were out of the rift and on the other side at Brazil Base. Mik and Bridger grabbed Torenz. Mik growled, "Cutting it a bit close, aren't you? It should go any second now."

They hustled to the large window she'd stood in front of so many times. The glass was missing and Charisse waited in a skimmer leveled right outside, a giant green sea of trees behind her. Farther out, two other skimmers filled with Jileah and her scientists were streaking away.

They dropped Torenz onto the floor of the skimmer and then climbed aboard. Mik took the controls and angled away from the window.

"What about our microchips?" Denefe asked Ardense.

"We arrested Hallen and have control of the

trigger."

Bridger pulled out a pressure hypodermic. "However, we don't know if someone has control of a second trigger. So, I'm going to remove your chips right away. Better safe than sorry. I'm going to dose you now so you're out when we land."

She nodded and clutched Ardense's hand. Fear crawled up and down her spine like some kind of wild animal. Why was she scared of the operation? She'd been through so much that was worse. Or at least it had seemed so.

She imagined she could feel the drug flowing through her. Her eyes immediately drooped and the focus of her world narrowed to just the skimmer. Dimly, she saw Bridger reach toward Kaleen's neck with another hypodermic.

The fog of the drug deepened, sucking her in. Somewhere behind the skimmer, a low buzz swelled. Rift spiders bit at her. She was aware of Mik saying, "Hold on everyone." Ardense wrapped his arms around her like a living seatbelt. Craning her neck, she fought to keep her eyes open and looked back at Brazil Base.

A blue bubble swelled like a balloon, engulfing the whole building, until it popped, sending shockwaves in all directions. The skimmer bucked and churned in the air. Then, as it settled into a smooth, driving rhythm, the drug took its final hold on her and she fell asleep.

* * * *

When Denefe opened her eyes, she was sure she'd only been asleep a few seconds and would wake still in the skimmer. Instead, she found herself in a hospital bed. Ardense was outside the room, speaking to someone about her. "…should be awake by now, don't you think?"

Another low voice answered. "She'll wake up when she's ready. There's nothing wrong. She's exhausted and needs sleep." Bridger?

Something made a shuffling noise to the right of her. Slowly turning, she saw Kaleen in a deep armchair, rubbing her arms and frowning at something in her hand. She looked at her sister's same white hair that matched hers, the heart-shaped face with the pouty mouth that laughed all too easy, and the petite frame that couldn't keep up. Happiness built a bubble in Denefe's heart. She was home.

"You look worried."

Kaleen whipped up her head and tears sprang to her eyes. She jumped to her feet and came close. "Welcome back! It's been a long twelve days." She squeezed Denefe's hand and smiled. Behind her, on the other side of the room, stretched Torenz's long, still body, handcuffed to the bed, two guards on either side of him. Denefe held her breath until she saw her brother's chest rise and fall with sleep.

She looked around the room. White austere walls. Small windows up high on the walls. The murmur of heavy cooling machines. Sterile smells. Shifting her focus back to Kaleen, she asked, "Where are we?"

"At Primary. As soon as we were all out, Bridger operated, right there in the seat of the shuttle, while Mik flew us here."

"What happened with the rift? I saw it explode. Were there many accidents?"

Kaleen's smile left. "There were so many sidewinders they're still charting them all. A lot of people were killed, but still, it was less than one-fourth of those who would have died had we allowed the rift to escalate." She opened Denefe's hand and placed something in it.

"A present?" Denefe lifted it and saw it was a

230

microchip, presumably from her own head. It looked strangely mangled on one side. Melted almost. She frowned and looked at her sister.

Kaleen locked her gaze onto Denefe. "It charged a miniature explosion maybe two minutes after Bridger removed it."

"So, there's someone with a second trigger."

"Was. Lieutenant Garza has him under arrest now too."

"Lieutenant Garza?"

"There's a lot to tell you."

"I guess. Is Torenz all right? Shouldn't he be waking now too?" Denefe struggled to sit, craning her neck to see him around her sister.

Kaleen pushed her back down on the bed. "We had to sedate him. He's been quite a handful."

"Don't I know it!"

Neither spoke for a moment. Denefe turned the chip over and over in her hand. She held it up against the light, studying the grooves and patterns. Finally, she said, "Kaleen, about Torenz…"

"He's our brother. I know. We'll be there for him. He'll have to face the consequences of his actions just like Hallen and the rest of his gang, but Lieutenant Garza is pretty sure he can convince Torenz to turn state's evidence." Kaleen leaned down and planted a kiss on Denefe's cheek. She got to her feet. "Now, I know a man who's been going crazy waiting for you to wake up."

A split-second after she left, Ardense's shadow filled the door of the room.

The End

231

Publisher's Note

Please help this author's career by posting an honest
review wherever you purchased this book.

About the Author

Wendy Koenig has been writing since a young child in Illinois, filling spirals with poetry and short stories. It wasn't until after a short stint in the military, that she began working on novels. It was also then that she began seeking publication.

Her first piece to be printed was a short children's fiction, *Jet's Stormy Adventure*, serialized in The Illinois Horse Network. She attended the University of Iowa, honing her craft in their famed summer workshops and writing programs. She graduated from the University of Maine, Presque Isle, in 2006. Her first novel was published in 2007. Since that time, she has published and co-authored numerous books.

Several of her story manuscripts have taken international awards: First Place Short Fiction and Second Place Novel in the 2005 Abilene Writers' Guild International Contest, Second Honorable Mention Novel in the 2005 CNW/FFWA International Writing Competition, and Second Honorable Mention Novel in the 2007 Frontiers in Writing International Contest.

Her short stories and poetry have appeared in multiple venues, including KidVisions ezine, Upcountry ezine, Echoes magazine, and the annual Breathe anthologies. She currently writes adult and Young Adult science fiction and action/adventure, as well as adult romance.

She currently lives in New Brunswick, Canada.

www.ingramcontent.com/pod-product-compliance
Lightning Source LLC
Chambersburg PA
CBHW071524110726
47908CB00003B/940